DESTRUCTION

THOR'S DRAGON RIDER

KATRINA COPE

COSY BURROW BOOKS

ASGARD'S DRAGON RIDER BOOKS

Valkyrie Academy Dragon Alliance
Series

Marked (Prequel)

Chosen

Vanished

Scorned

Inflicted

Empowered

Ambushed

Warned

Abducted

Besieged

Deceived

Thor's Dragon Rider Series

Safeguard

Pursuit

Entrapment

Hoodwinked

Relinquished

Shrouded

Assigned

Accosted

Destruction

EDITORIAL REVIEW

Thor's Dragon Rider
Book Nine

Destruction

"As the forces of darkness invade Asgard, Kara faces the loss of everything she loves. The unexpected twists and nonstop action of this thrilling tale will please readers old and new." Irene S., Proofreader, Red Adept Editing

"Destruction is filled with quick-witted dragons, plenty of action, commanding heroines, and complex villains who may be anything but villainous." - Stefanie B., Red Adept Editing Line Editor

Destruction

Ebook first published in USA in July 2022 by Cosy Burrow Books

Ebook first published in Great Britain in July 2022 by Cosy Burrow Books

www.katrinacopebooks.com

Text Copyright © 2022 by Katrina Cope

Cover Design Copyright © art4artists.com.au

Published by Cosy Burrow Books

ISBN : 978-0-6455102-1-8

BLURB

Hideous darkness dampens Asgard as the predicted doom looms.

The World Tree is meant to be the bringer of life to the Norse realms, yet the access from the other worlds may be Asgard's undoing. The hideous monsters from the under realms climb through the trunk's opening, bearing Hel's wrath. Asgard, its occupants, and many of the other realms are in significant danger from the monsters, combined with the threat of the Midgard serpent and Fenrir.

As their friends place their lives at risk, Kara and Elan work to gather more fighters before putting themselves in war's peril. Will their efforts save Asgard and their friends, or is it too late?

Chapter One

S pear in hand, Odin approaches the growling hound. Fenrir lurches, pulling at his lead and stretching it farther. The hound seems to have grown even since Hildr and I removed the stick prying open his jaw. His vast array of teeth is fully displayed as his mouth spreads wide and he hovers only a few feet away, towering over Odin. Fenrir's matted fur stands on end down his spine, and his tether thins. The hound is nearly twice the god's height, yet Odin seems undeterred.

Still hiding behind the boulder, I watch, assessing the situation taking place on part of Asgard's large rocky plain surrounded by boulders. The brilliant blue sky contradicts the mood playing out before me. I thought Odin was coming here to check if Fenrir was still on his lead. Fenrir remains secured by Gleipnir, leaving me wondering why Odin continues to approach the hound, tempting his fate.

Fenrir's lips retract farther, and he jerks harder against the lead. Slobber cascades from his mouth, and he shakes his head, flinging drool in all directions. Some lands on the boulder next to where I stand. My nose screws in distaste, but I refuse to let this take my focus away from the god and the hound.

"Behave, you monstrous beast," Odin cries then swings Gungnir, striking Fenrir's snout with the spear's shaft. Odin's two ravens circle around the hound and descend to land on Odin's shoulders as he brushes the gray strands of hair from covering his one good eye.

The hound pulls at his lead, growling and snapping, desperate to get at the god. His paws slip slightly on a few small stones scattered on the hard surface between them. Odin remains just out of reach and adjusts his black eye patch as one of the ravens snuggles close to his ear.

"Why don't you come closer?" Fenrir taunts the god. "Or are you too chicken?"

Odin beats the hound across his paw. "I am not afraid of you. You need to learn how to behave. That is why I'm here."

Lifting his injured paw, Fenrir chomps and tears at the lead before pushing forward, stretching Gleipnir to its limits. Despite being infused by dwarven magic and made from special ingredients to prevent breaking, the restraint stretches so thin, I'm not sure it's going to hold.

Holding back a gasp of shock, I remain hiding behind the boulder. The way Odin is going, he will be responsible for Fenrir's release all because he aggravated him too much. A small bird swoops past, surprising me by narrowly missing my ear before landing on a nearby boulder. I would think the bird should be put off by the commotion between the god and the hound.

Blind to the danger, Odin doesn't relent. He laughs at the hound's attempts, annoying the hound more. My cheeks turn clammy. The situation is no laughing matter.

Odin's ravens, Huginn and Muninn, take flight and attack Fenrir. Their efforts disturb the hound more, distracting him. He writhes and snaps at the ravens, snatching some of their black tail feathers between his teeth. The hound shakes the feathers from his mouth and shifts, ready to try again.

Odin whacks the hound again across his snout to distract him from the birds. "I'm going to stop the prophecy. I'm not going to let you destroy Asgard and bring on Ragnarok. You will fall before you get the chance." His wrinkles fold on themselves as he scowls deeply and wallops the hound again.

Fenrir stops attacking the ravens and stares at

Odin, a deep growl rumbling up his throat. "I'm not interested in Ragnarok. I'm only interested in ending your life and anybody else responsible for trapping my father."

I attempt to swallow the lump in my throat. Surely Odin will listen to the hound and leave him alone.

The god slams Gungnir's shaft across the hound's foreleg. "Don't you lie to me! The prophecies are never wrong about your intentions. But I will change the result of their prediction. You won't be my downfall. I'm too mighty to be brought down by a mere hound. You don't stand a chance to bring on Ragnarok."

Fenrir growls. "I told you I'm not interested in starting Ragnarok. Although I promise you that you are definitely in my sights. You have a lot to pay for."

Odin's actions are not only barbaric, but also stupid, and it makes me wonder how he is called the wise god. He sacrificed his eye in exchange for a drink from Mimir's well, which gave him wisdom. And the rumors say he carries around Mimir's head to continue to seek his knowledge. Still, Odin has the potential to be quite stupid.

"What's the matter? Are you stuck on your restraint, you poor little hound?"

Fenrir reels forward, dragging the immense

boulder securing his restraint. Gleipnir is stretched to the utmost limit. I don't know how it hasn't snapped already. Odin is here under the pretense of stopping Fenrir's escape. Instead, he may be the reason for the hound's freedom.

The god moves quickly, swiping his spear shaft up underneath Fenrir's chin and knocking his teeth together. The hound's head tilts upwards briefly, and when he lowers it, the hatred in his eyes is far more than I've seen before. It scares me to imagine what this hound is planning. He is intelligent as well as ferocious.

Facing the glaring hound, Odin simply laughs as though he's mocking him, making him angrier. "Do you think you're going to be able to scare me with a simple growl and fire in your eyes? I am the god of all gods and leader of Asgard. You cannot scare me like that. It will take a lot more than that to worry me."

I want to intervene, but Odin doesn't listen to me. Nearly every time I've suggested something, he's dismissed it or belittled me. Yet I can see the danger in the hound's eyes, and it causes my nerves to fire. I edge forward, and the same tiny bird swoops in front of me, startling me into a halt before disappearing out of sight.

Odin swings Gungnir again, narrowly missing

Fenrir, who dodges the strike. The god brings his spear back again, smacking him across the chin. The ravens caw and attack Fenrir's ears.

The hound snaps and pulls, growling and hissing, drool coming out everywhere. The boulder restraining Fenrir inches forward. Odin takes a couple of steps back, but the hound doesn't relent. He has gone beyond his patience, not that he had any in the first place. His attack on Odin intensifies, and his fury shines through. Each of the god's attacks stokes the hound's ferocity, and he drags the boulder forward. The lead slowly creeps underneath the boulder.

I hate the cruelty that Odin is giving this hound, causing me to think he will deserve whatever punishment Fenrir prescribes him. I'm about to approach Odin when Fenrir pulls again, causing the boulder behind him to rock precariously. It's about to tip and release the hound. I hold back, not wanting to succumb to the hound's jaws along with the god. I would be useless to Odin if the hound devours me first. Just then, Fenrir rears back then lunges forward with enough force to topple the boulder, releasing the lead.

Chapter Two

O din staggers backward, attempting to evade the strike, and trips on a rock. His backside hits the ground with a padded thud, his burgundy cloak folding and cushioning his landing. Fenrir's mouth narrowly misses him. The god rolls to climb to his feet, resorting to all fours when he fails to rise in time. A rare display of panic fills Odin's face as Fenrir lunges at him again. Odin dodges to the side, shaving past the snap of the hound's teeth.

Fenrir charges at the fallen god, his lead trailing behind him. Odin swerves to the side another time, still clambering on all fours. Fenrir's teeth snatch the top of Odin's cloak, and Odin dangles as the hound shakes him violently. Drool flies in all directions. Odin kicks and punches at the hound, unable to reach significant spots.

I move from around the boulder and approach Fenrir. Fully aware that Fenrir hates me also, I have little faith I can stop him from killing Odin. Spotting me, Fenrir halts, concentrating his glare on me. He growls before asking through clenched teeth still clasping the god's cloak, "What do you want?"

I approach ever so slowly, making sure I'm still out of reach of the snapping jaws. "I come in peace, Fenrir," I say with the most respectful voice I can muster despite my apprehension. "I understand that Odin has taunted you and that it's made you angry." I cast a sideways glance at Odin and continue. "And undoubtedly, he has provoked you. If I'm truthful, I would say that he deserves the treatment you're giving him now."

I catch the disdainful look from Odin and ignore it. I'm only speaking the truth, and he's not exactly in a commanding position right now.

"My furry butt, he deserves it!" Fenrir's teeth tighten on Odin's cloak. "I should tear him to pieces right now."

I inch slightly closer and work on stopping my knees from quivering. "Please reconsider. After the treatment he has given you, your anger is perfectly understandable. But if you do that, it will condemn you for life. You'll have many enemies that will hunt you to the ends of the nine realms. They won't stop until they make you pay."

Fenrir shakes the god like a ragdoll again before

releasing him and sending him flying several feet away. Odin grunts as he lands with a thump after slamming against a boulder. He moans as he tries to roll, probably dealing with deep bruises and maybe some broken bones.

Fenrir sneers at Odin before towering over me. "I don't care if they hunt me to the ends of the earth. He needs to pay for what he has done."

I crane my neck to look up at his face. "Wouldn't you rather live the end of your life in peace, especially with the Asgardians? Maybe you can befriend Tyr again. You two used to be so close."

The hound's brown eyes soften briefly after the mention of Tyr then sharpen on me. "I wish to punish many people in this realm for what they have done to my father, and you are one of them." He leans forward, and his matted fur stands on end, making him seem larger, dwarfing me.

Odin climbs to his feet, grabs Gungnir, and darts at the hound, swinging at the hound's head. "You'll die before you hurt any Asgardians."

Fenrir spins toward Odin, and I whip up a magical barrier, separating the two. The hound jumps and snaps at Odin, attempting to push through the barrier.

The hound notices my raised hands and growls at me. "Let me through!"

Shaking my head, I say, "I'm afraid I can't do that. Despite Odin doing stupid things to you, I can't let you hurt him or kill him. I wouldn't be doing my job if I did."

Odin swings his spear at the hound again, but the barrier blocks his strike. The god looks at me, curses, then demands, "Let me at him."

At first, his retort makes me cringe, and my strength to deny him returns only when I remember why I came to find him. I straighten my shoulders. "You have much better uses elsewhere, great leader. I respect you and your wishes, but I'm not obeying your demand this time. You taunting the hound is only making the situation worse. We need your help to organize the armies. Asgard is under attack. Fenrir isn't the only one angered. Jormungandr has made his way onto the realm. Not only that, Hel has sent several lava monsters and draugar, and who knows what else will appear. All of them are attacking us on our land."

Odin's face pales. He stands dumbfounded, staring up at Fenrir's snapping jaws, blocked by only my magic barrier.

When he doesn't respond, I continue, my jaw tight with tension. "I need you to go back to the palace and organize all the Valkyries and the gods fit for war. They need to find my friends with the dragons near the entrance of Yggdrasil. There are only three Valkyries and their dragons fighting the lava giants and the draugar, and they need help. They don't have a chance against all of them. Elan has gone to get her dragon family from the wastelands to help Thor against the Midgard serpent."

When he still doesn't move, I cry out, "Please! Forget Fenrir and go and do this. I'm not trying to tell you what to do, but Asgard needs your help! Everything you have said that will be happening to cause Ragnarok is happening. We need you to focus, not taunt some hound you predicted will be your downfall. If you act now, you may be able to avoid the outcome you have seen in your mind's eye with all your great wisdom. Now's the time for you to take charge and do what you were born to do."

Fenrir growls. "He can't do that. I'm not finished with him yet. I'm going to put an end to this terrible god, and then I'm going to end you." He sneers at me. "If you don't let me through now, I will attack you first, destroying your hold over the magic barrier, and then I will get him."

I expel an audible sigh. "I have no doubt you wish to kill both of us, Fenrir. But I'm not going to release my barrier so you can attack Odin. If you wish to kill him, you'll have to do it through me first."

Odin looks from the hound to me then back at the hound before spinning on his heels. His ravens land on his shoulders as he heads back to the palace.

"Let me at him!" Fenrir growls, watching the god disappear.

I shake my head. "I'm sorry, Fenrir. I can't do that."

"Then, like I promised, it's you I will destroy first. I've wanted to get my teeth into you for a very long time." He stalks forward, padding toward me. His massive paws make no sound against the rocks as he inches closer. He doesn't pound or jump at me. He just takes his time. Each footstep he takes is probably three of my own, if not more. As I stare up at this massive beast that used to be the cutest puppy I'd ever seen, I'm saddened that it has come to this. I know that I have not one scrap of chance to outrun him.

Chapter Three

Holding up my hands, I construct a magic barrier and back away, fully aware I won't be able to hold up my defense forever. "I know you're upset, Fenrir, but please, there's a lot more at stake than you just being upset over your father." The second those words leave my mouth, I know I've made a mistake.

A sparrow flies around my head, irritating me, but I can't take my eyes off the approaching hound, growling and ready to pounce. "I'm sorry. That's not what I meant. What I mean is, can't we just talk about this and deal with it later?"

"Like I'm going to give you any more chances," Fenrir snarls. "You've taken my father away from me for no reason. He did nothing."

Even though Loki has caused a lot of grief and betrayed Asgard, I don't want to go into that with his angry son, especially right now. "Fenrir, if we don't stop your sister's and brother's attack, you may not have a realm to live on."

"As much as I don't appreciate my serpent brother, I trust Hel's instincts, which deem this realm guilty," Fenrir says. "I will find another realm to live on. This realm means nothing to me."

Continuing my slow retreat, I ask, "What about Tyr? He has raised you from a pup, and he loves you like his own."

"I will protect Tyr as much as I can, although I'm sure he won't need my help. He is a warrior god, a god of war. One who is battle-hardened and able to protect himself." The hound's eyes display very little empathy.

I'm shocked by the lack of compassion when he speaks of his guardian. "But you removed one of these arms, remember? He only has one arm to fight with now."

"And that is the gods' fault," Fenrir growls. "If they hadn't tricked me into this lead, Tyr would still have his arm. I had to show the gods that I'm not to be walked over, and Tyr understands that."

I back up a few more steps. My talking to him isn't getting through. My mind whirls with a way to try to calm the hound. Thanks to Odin, he's ready to destroy anything in his path. The bird circles my face again. I long to swipe it away, yet I don't want my barrier to falter or create any sudden movements to provoke Fenrir to attack.

A thought comes to my head. "Fenrir, did you realize your father has escaped many times?"

The hound doesn't respond, although I think I see a glimpse of uncertainty in his eyes, wiped away within moments.

I continue. "He was originally chained up and secured by magic leads, but he escaped. Some of it was thanks to me. I must admit it wasn't my intention for him to escape, but I did release him to help with something. Since then, he has been in and out of capture without Odin knowing, many times." I eye the hound, hoping the truth will sink in and calm his aggression. "Your father has been doing all sorts of things again, like tricking me, and has agreed to go back into enclosure again. Just recently, he agreed on his own to stay there until we had finished collecting tears for Balder in an attempt to release the god from your sister's grasp."

"You lie!" Fenrir snarls. "I will never believe you with anything. My father wasn't free. You captured him, and it's your fault he is suffering."

Fenrir lunges for me, and I reinforce the strength of my magic barrier.

He collides with it, making him more frustrated.

Snarling, he claws at it and pushes against the boundary, the magic lead still trailing behind him.

"You're cheating!" Fenrir screams.

"I'm merely protecting myself," I say calmly. "You won't listen to my reason, and I don't want to fight you or hurt you. I know you're upset, and I get that. But I wish you would just move on and let me help the others protect Asgard."

"You don't deserve to protect Asgard. You don't deserve to stay alive. You deserve to be killed by my teeth." Drool drips from the hound's mouth.

I can feel my strength weakening. This hound is strong, and this barrier takes all of my effort. Trying to hold it there, especially after having held one for Odin for so long, seems to be draining me quicker.

Fenrir keeps pushing at the boundary, and it bends a little, robbing me of more energy when I have to straighten it. Beads of sweat trickle off my forehead, and I wipe them on my sleeve, making sure I keep my hands firmly in place. The hound pushes through the boundary slightly, and I move back a couple of paces.

Grunting against the strain, I say, "I swear I'm telling the truth. Your father has escaped many times and could probably escape now if he wanted to. He's only there because he made an agreement."

The breeze blows from behind Fenrir, pushing the

smell of dirty dog in my direction, and I screw up my nose. The hound has been restrained for a long time and could use a good bath. He probably feels disgusting with oils and fats clinging to his fur, making him more irritable. I wouldn't be surprised if the gods had skipped feeding him meals in an attempt to stop his growth because he's getting too big.

He pushes forward again, and I gasp, trying to hold the barrier. My arms are exhausted. Even so, I have to keep it up. If the hound breaks through, I don't like my chances of defeating him all by myself. I pull from my buried strength and toughen my reserve. If I don't, it'll most likely be the end of me. Still, my strength is wavering, and I can't see myself lasting much longer. Being killed by Fenrir wasn't how I saw my ending. I hoped that if I passed, I'd be protecting Asgard. Instead, I'm protecting myself, and this saddens me. Fenrir isn't interested in destroying Asgard. He's only interested in punishing the people who locked up his father.

I pull from within again, attempting to gather all my hidden strength down to the dregs of my stomach. I'm not going to give up now.

I hear the flapping of wings and catch sight of the small bird flying around Fenrir's ears. Fenrir pulls back his teeth and snaps at the sparrow, and the bird dodges to the side. He snaps again when the bird comes closer, encircling the sparrow within his teeth. I'm certain the bird is dead until its tiny form weaves through a gap in the hound's teeth. The bird pushes into the air, and irritation grows in the hound's eyes.

I brace myself, ready for Fenrir to take his frustration out on me, then something catches my attention. Wiping the sweat from my forehead with my sleeve, I quickly glance out the corner of my eye right as the sparrow morphs into Loki.

Bewilderment is pasted over the mischievous god's face as he smooths down his black leather coat that flows to his calves. "Oh, my son! That was close. You nearly ate me." Loki gives the hound a look of disbelief before brushing back his black shoulder-length hair to reveal a smirk of amusement covering his pointy face as he looks at his son.

Fenrir's eyes widen. "Father?"

"Well, who else would it be?" Loki says, spreading his arms out to the sides. Fenrir charges along the side of the barrier to the gap before nudging his father with his nose.

I release any barrier between them and move to a safe distance.

Chapter Four

Fenrir drops his aggressiveness as Loki embraces his son in a big hug around his head. My heart melts when I see joy wash over the hound's face.

Loki rubs Fenrir around the ears, and the hound's tongue drops out to the side. "What she said is true, Fenrir," Loki says. "I have escaped many times. Don't take your aggression out on Kara. She was merely protecting Asgard, and I kind of deserved my punishment." Loki shrugs, looking sheepish.

"But she's the reason you were locked up." Fenrir scowls my way. "She should pay for making you be locked up. That's not very nice."

Loki strokes his snout. "It was her duty. And she wasn't the only one. She was the nice one locking me up, and we could do with some more nice people." Loki nudges Fenrir's side, and the hound looks at him then back at me before returning his gaze to his father as though trying to assess if he was serious. "And she stopped you from being attacked by Odin."

"More like she stopped *me* from attacking Odin," Fenrir says. "I want to rip his throat out for what he's done to you and me."

Loki chuckles. "You and me both, but that will only land us in more hot water." He hugs Fenrir a couple more times, squeezing him around the neck. And it's nice to see the hound's face relaxed, almost turning back into the cute puppy again. "So, what do you say? Are we going to leave Kara alone?" He rubs Fenrir's ears again. "I wish you would. Because I've grown quite fond of her."

I frown at his comment. The number of times this god has betrayed me is beyond ridiculous. A strangled noise of disbelief escapes my mouth.

Loki peers back at me and shrugs. "I'm telling the truth."

"Now, that would be a first," I say.

Loki feigns hurt. "Oh, so harsh."

I glower at the god. He causes my mind and heart to run through so many emotions, it's ridiculous. I don't know which way is up or down.

Loki turns to Fenrir. "Why don't you go over and give her a hug?"

"You know I love you, Father. But that's not

something I'm about to do," Fenrir says.

Not sure how I'd feel having Fenrir that close to me with his massive jaws near my body, I say, "I'm happy with that response."

Seeing my resistance, Loki gives up on the idea, and he throws an arm around Fenrir's neck and whispers in his ear loudly enough that I can hear. "I hear you don't like your brother, Jormungandr. Why don't you take all that anger and go and help them fight him? He's trying to cause havoc on Asgard, and he could wreck this realm." Loki tightens his half hug on the hound. "I heard he gave you quite a hard time when you were a pup before you were separated. Now you might want to get back at him, and it's a perfect opportunity to get rid of all that frustration welled up inside." Loki pulls back and smiles, showing Fenrir all of his straight white teeth.

Fenrir's ears prick up. "I like that idea." Fenrir licks his father's hand. "You're right. He was always nasty to me when I was a pup."

I'm amazed at how differently Fenrir takes the news about his serpent brother attacking Asgard from his father compared to when I told him. I push it aside. Of course he's going to listen to his father before me. Loki hasn't told Fenrir precisely what he will be up against. Maybe Loki doesn't even know.

"Just a little warning," I say. "The Midgard

serpent is huge."

"Haven't you seen me?" Fenrir asks, standing at full height, towering over me, at least double my size.

Nodding, I agree, "I've definitely seen you. You're huge too, but nothing in comparison to the size of Jormungandr."

"But you said that all the dragons from the waste-land are coming too, didn't you?" Loki asks.

"Yes, if what Elan does is successful, the dragons will be coming from the wasteland to help Thor protect Asgard from Jormungandr."

Loki pets Fenrir's leg. "There you go. You've got plenty of help. Why don't you go and make use of that?"

The hound takes off without waiting for another prompt, his nose twitching as he sniffs to catch his brother's scent.

I watch the hound leave, my feet fixed to the spot, and I'm too shocked to speak. He went without snap-ping or threatening me. Loki has completely changed the hound's attitude. It's been ages since I've seen Fenrir so happy. He has been so nasty lately, and that's all I've come to expect from him.

"What just happened?" I ask.

Loki smirks at me. "Why, I just saved your life again. You're welcome." He follows Fenrir.

After pausing for a moment, I hurry to catch up with him. "Hang on. You said you would stay locked up until we got all the tears for Balder." I grab him by the upper arm and turn him to look at me. "You lied again."

A grin spreads over Loki's face. "You shouldn't make a bargain with a trickster."

I scowl and place my hands on my hips. "So you admit you lied?"

The god shakes his head, looking quite smug. "I didn't lie, and I didn't break our bargain."

"But you did," I say. "You're out free. You've escaped from your cell, and we didn't get the tears for Balder."

"My dear Kara. You should listen more carefully to the words that you agree to." The grin on his face taunts me. "I agreed that when you had finished collecting tears for Balder, I would escape from my cell. Not when you collected all the tears for Balder."

The realization hits me hard. He hasn't broken his promise. He merely made sure his words were just right so he could twist them when he wanted to. He probably knew we would never get all the tears for Balder.

"No wonder they call you the trickster." Spite lines my voice, but at the same time, I can't hold it against him because this time, he did nothing wrong.

"At your service." Loki bows mockingly before turning and continuing on his way.

With hurried footsteps, I follow him. "Where are you going now?"

"I'm going to assess the situation and see what I want to do."

"So you're not going to help us from the generosity of your heart?" I ask. "You're going to see if you want to help us."

Loki nods. "That's the way it should go." When he spots my frown, he asks, "What's wrong with that?"

"It's so selfish. That's what's wrong with that."

He shrugs, and the leather of his jacket squeaks. "Well, that's the life of being around me. That's the reputation I have, and that's the reputation I uphold. I have no regrets." His steps falter. "Well, maybe a couple. I've been quite bad." He peers at me from the side. "I'm still not committing yet."

I grunt. "You are so frustrating!" I want to scream the words but settle for saying them through my teeth. After a brief pause, I ask, "Don't you have any sympathy or empathy for your brother?"

"Do you mean my blood brother, Odin?"

I nod.

"That would be a definite no." He looks like he thinks for a moment. "For Thor? Possibly."

Chapter Five

I stare at Loki's back as I follow him toward the area of the Midgard serpent. I can't contain my puzzlement any longer. "Why did you just help me?"

Loki calls over his shoulder, "Do you mean help protect you from being eaten by my son?"

Distracted by his brazenness, I trip over a rock. "Yes. That would be the first thing that comes to mind."

He pauses and turns to face me. "You sound puzzled that I would help you."

Stopping in front of him, I cross my arms. "You're not exactly the most trustworthy person."

He lifts his raven eyebrow as he looks at me before continuing his journey to his serpent son. "Believe it or not, Kara, I like you. And I don't want any harm to come to you." Palm up, he waves his arm out to the side. "I believe I've told this to you before, but obviously, you don't believe me."

I scramble to keep up with him then block his path. "Why would I believe you? You seem to do everything possible to go against us. You've tricked me that many times. You deceived me. You've gone against Asgard. And then you go and get Balder killed by deceiving Hodr."

Loki shrugs. "I am not responsible for Hodr's actions."

Thrusting my arms out wide, I groan. "Ah. But you are. You found the only thing that could hurt Balder, then manipulated his blind brother to aim the mistletoe weapon directly at his heart. You used his blindness and his longing to join in on the fun to kill his own brother. Thanks to you, Hodr couldn't live with himself. That's low. Hodr thought his brother was invincible and nothing could harm him."

"Then he should have been smarter."

My mouth drops open. "That is exactly why I don't trust you. One minute, you say you like people and want to help them. The next minute, you go against everything, purposely disrupting things."

Loki's face remains unchanged. "Everything I do has a purpose."

"Yes, to protect yourself," I snap. "All you ever think about is yourself."

Loki's eyebrows twitch. "Then why did I protect you against Fenrir?"

My words get stuck in my throat. I have nothing to answer with. I don't understand why he protected me from Fenrir. The part where he tells me he did it because he likes me doesn't resonate.

We continue toward Jormungandr in silence. I decide not to challenge him anymore. It sounds like we could use his help if he has any influence over his children. Perhaps he does, or maybe he doesn't. There is no harm in taking his help unless he's going to betray us again. I'll have to keep an extra eye on him. As far as I know, he hasn't been stealing dragon eggs anymore and hasn't drummed up a secret army of dragons ridden by dwarf giants like he did last time we thought it was Ragnarok. Yet this time, other predictions in play are coming true, causing me to believe this is more like Ragnarok than the other battle on Asgard ever was. Although the other realms are very beautiful, Asgard is our home, and I don't want to see it destroyed. Not only that, but if Asgard falls, it will unbalance the World Tree and destroy other realms, possibly all six of the middle and upper realms. Yggdrasil might even die. I'm not sure the under realms need Yggdrasil to survive. Their realms are almost dead.

As we walk, I search the skies, looking for the dragons from the wastelands. Worry niggles my stomach when I can't see them. I hope Elan gets to them quickly and they agree to come. We need their help. A large flock of winged Valkyries passes over the top, their high-pitched war cry screaming through the air, giving me hope that we have assistance. They swoop low over us, and one of them lands in front of me, poised for combat.

Affronted, I shuffle back a couple of paces before I look up and see my once nemesis from the Valkyrie Academy. Warmth washes over me when I realize the reasoning behind Rota's aggressive stance.

Her pretty blue eyes turn icy as she studies Loki. "Are you okay, Kara? Is this deceptive god annoying you?" She draws her sword, her fingers twitching with keenness to attack the traitor of Asgard. It's still strange seeing this Valkyrie wanting to protect me after everything she did to me in the Valkyrie Academy.

She's swapped her battle uniform of tanned leather jacket, plain white T-shirt, and long medium-blue pants for black fighting leathers. Another change that the wingless Valkyries have influenced. Her pure blond hair is pulled back into a ponytail, with a few strands falling loose along her pale cheeks.

With a pleasant expression plastered on his face, Loki faces her. "My dear Valkyrie. Of course she's fine with me." His voice is filled with false innocence. "I'm her favorite god."

Resisting a snort, I roll my eyes. "I'm fine. Thank you, Rota. I'm just escorting Loki toward the battle scene his monster children have brought to Asgard. He says he wants to help. Although, I could use your help to keep an eye on him. We all know how trustworthy he is."

She stares at Loki for a while, taking him in and assessing his face as though analyzing an enemy's next move.

When she doesn't say anything, I add, "I hope the dragons from the wasteland will be here soon, and when they come, I assume I'll be distracted."

Her mouth flattens into a thin line. "I'll be happy to keep an eye on him. Naturally, I'll be fighting, but I'll watch him every second I have."

Loki grins. "How lovely to have so much attention from beautiful women."

Rota's eyes narrow. "Don't flatter yourself. I wouldn't trust you if you were the last person on the realms."

I huff. "I'm one hundred percent with you, Rota."

The corners of Loki's mouth turn down as he feigns hurt. I ignore him.

Rota pushes off into the air with her sword in hand and joins her Valkyrie battle maidens. The shrill

Valkyrie battle cry follows her, joining the cries of the other Valkyries and the roars of the lava monsters in the distance. I hope Zildryss, all the large dragons and their riders are fine. Those Valkyries have stood by my side from the start, and it would destroy me if something happened to them.

Either Loki's pace has slackened, or my anxiousness is growing. "Can't we hurry it up a bit? I can't stand the thought of all my friends fighting these monsters without me. At the moment, the odds aren't in their favor."

"My dear Kara."

I prickle over the patronizing tone.

Loki holds up a calming hand. "I could tell you were running out of magic back there. You need to recoup. Have a drink." He holds out a magically produced cup. "Or a snack." His other hand holds magically created nuts. "You'll need everything you have, physically, mentally, and magically, back in your stores."

He knows me too well, and thanks to his constant deceptiveness, I hardly know him at all. I glare at him. "I'm fine."

My teacher of magic holds the cup and nuts closer to me. "I beg to differ, and that worries me. I'm merely looking after your health and potential to succeed in this battle."

Snatching the drink and nuts, I grumble, "You don't know me as well as you think." I down the drink and pop a nut into my mouth. "My power will have regenerated by the time we get there because you're walking so slowly." I throw more nuts into my mouth.

The god watches me eating his supplies with a look of knowing he won this point, yet he doesn't brag. "And that's exactly my point. That's the reason I'm taking my time."

As I finish my nuts, my steps quicken, and I growl, "Hurry up."

Loki's pace slows further, and a satisfied smirk fills his face. "Or what? You could go ahead without me."

I groan with frustration. I know he won over the food, beverage, and rest, yet at the same time, I know I should be keeping an eye on him. But the battle and my friends' safety worry me more. I jog toward the area where we last left Thor with Jormungandr.

Lightning strikes the sky and bounces back to the ground, alerting me to exactly where Thor is fighting the Midgard serpent alone until the dragons arrive. I hope Fenrir is helping, even though the two combined aren't going to be enough to fight that monstrous thing. The prophecy has Thor battling the serpent, but he needs help, or the serpent could be the one that finishes Thor.

Dark clouds form above, and more lightning shoots from them, bouncing to and from the clouds and ground.

A sparrow morphs into Loki just in front of me. My breath stilted from jogging, I scowl at his ability to cheat the distance.

"You're going to be out of breath before you even get there," he says, his breath heavy but not as ragged as mine. He falls into pace a step behind me.

I straighten my shoulders and hide my struggle to breathe. "If you can't keep up, then don't try. You don't need to make excuses by saying it's me who doesn't have the energy. I'm much fitter than you. I've had all the training of a Valkyrie."

Loki's steps quicken, and his breathing grows more labored. "Fine. If you insist on keeping up this pace, I will have to change again." He turns into a small bird again and flies farther ahead.

I quicken my pace, stumbling as I try to keep up with him, and my breath grows more ragged. Ahead, lightning hits the sky another time, sending out a loud crack followed by thunder.

Chapter Six

"Wow, that's impressive." Loki's feet halt as he eyes the serpent rearing up, ready to attack Thor. "I had no idea Jormungandr turned out so big." Eyes wide, the mischievous god watches his giant son strike at Thor.

Hearing a loud growl from the other side of the giant serpent, I jump just as Fenrir pounces from behind a boulder and sinks his teeth into Jormungandr's flesh. The serpent hisses in pain and rears up, dragging the hound up with him. Fenrir releases his grip and lands on the ground, poised on all fours.

With Mjollnir held high, Thor shoots lightning into the sky then aims the lightning at the serpent. Jormungandr shifts to the side at the last moment. The lightning skimming his skin as it passes. The hiss he expels sends shivers down my spine as he snakes his head, ready to strike the god of thunder.

Loki whistles then shifts next to me. "I'm not

exactly a fan of Thor, but he is better than Odin. I'll see if I can stop him from being attacked." He surprises me by breaking into a light jog toward the serpent.

My gaze wanders to the dragons fighting the lava monsters. My dragon friends and riders look lonely fighting the enormous creatures, even though the winged Valkyries are prepping to attack. Worry gnaws at my stomach. The dragons almost look defenseless until I spot Zildryss landing on the ground. The little dragon shoots the tip of his tail into the ground like a scorpion, burying the monsters up to their necks. The stifled monsters roar and spew lava, trying to catch someone in the scalding mass. It's surprising to see the smallest dragon conducting the most effective move to combat these invaders. Yet his efforts seem fruitless as more monsters file out of the World Tree's trunk. There are too many monsters for the small group of defenders.

My heart sinks when I watch the devastation created by these monsters. Naga dives with Eir on his back. She has magic cupped in one hand and a sword in the other. The peaceful Valkyrie and dragon are fighting along with the others in a losing battle.

The winged Valkyries fire arrows in unison at one monster. Many arrows hit the monster's rough stone-like exterior and fall to the ground, while the fiery pits of lava consume the other arrows. The winged Valkyries then throw their swords. Several pierce the cracks and into the monsters, but the lava's heat melts the blades.

I scan the horizon. There is no sign of Odin's rescue teams consisting of gods and einherjar. Surely Odin hasn't taken my warning lightly and has executed the demand for the gods and warriors to fight as well as the Valkyries. The Valkyries have the advantage of speed with their ability to fly to the battle. Reminding myself of this helps me believe Odin's armies must be on their way.

More lava monsters and draugar enter Asgard. The sight is horrifying. Even if the warriors are coming, we need more help. The armies we have on Asgard aren't going to be enough. Surely all of this is not simply because Idun insulted Hel with her offer of youth and beauty. There must be a deeper stem to this hatred of Asgard and its occupants.

Tanda swoops in front of a lava monster, spewing fire. The effort is commendable, yet I doubt flames will do anything to a beast already based on fire. Britta hurls magic at the monster, but it doesn't seem to affect the beast.

The lava monster swipes a hand, and claws swipe the back of Tanda's rear. The red dragon roars in pain, sending chills down my spine. Her body falls with Britta on her back, and worry turns my gut to a sickly mush. It was the strike of a lava monster that nearly killed Elan. The poison under its claws didn't work instantly, but it weakened her until she could no longer function. I watch the red dragon worriedly, hoping the monster didn't get any poison under her scales and cut her skin. Moments later, Tanda gains control of her momentum and steadies her flight to rejoin the battle. The lava monster swipes at her again from the other direction.

I search the skies for my beautiful dragon, only to find a vacant sky. There isn't a single dragon from the wastelands heading our way. I bite my lip, worried for my bonded friend, and remind myself that the travel from the wastelands is far.

Zildryss circles the monster attacking Tanda before landing on the ground. He pokes his tail straight into the ground. The lava monster swipes for the little dragon, missing when his body sinks deep into Asgard's surface mid-stride, leaving only the head of the lava monster above the ground. It spews lava toward Zildryss, and the tiny dragon narrowly dodges to the side.

The draugar slip past my friends and the winged Valkyries' defenses, plaguing the land and heading straight for the palace. Their direction is spot on, and I wonder if they are controlled directly by Hel's memory from her brief visit to Asgard, or if they have a sixth sense of where to go.

If Hel is truly upset by Odin, her hate for him must have originated in the palace. The draugar are pouring through Yggdrasil's trunk faster than the lava monsters. Soon they will outnumber our armies. We need more help. We need to contact the other realms somehow. I scan the very distant branches of the World Tree. The Yggdrasil is too far away to search the branches successfully for Ratatoskr. The other branch of the Yggdrasil that opens onto Asgard near the palace is also too far away to search for the squirrel. There is no chance of calling the messenger in time to gather help.

A roar shrills, and I spin quickly to check for danger. My arrows rattle loudly in the quiver on my back, and I remember the charm Freya gave me when I was at the Valkyrie Academy. I pull my quiver off my back and search its sides. When I see the small silver charm with a cornet lying across a set of wings dangling from a loop on my quiver, relief floods my body. Holding it in my fingers, I rub my thumb across the hard surface, feeling the indents of the sculpturing. I'd forgotten it was there, although I didn't need it until now. It had become part of my accessories.

Kara. It's been a long time. Freya's sensually feminine voice instantly projects into my head, causing me to jump. *Do you need something or have secret army information for me?* She pauses. *Please don't tell me you're stuck on Muspelheim again.*

"Freya, thank you for contacting me back so quickly. No, I'm not stuck on Muspelheim, but we need the help of your angels of death. Hel is attacking Asgard, and I believe it may be the start of Ragnarok." Before she protests, I add, "This time more than last time. Hel has sent her minions to attack, and the Midgard serpent is attacking Thor on Asgard. Also, Fenrir has escaped. I think his aggression is tempered for now, but I can't be sure. He may still attack Odin later or during the battle." I clutch the charm tighter. "We need your help. This battle makes the last one look tame."

Without hesitation, Freya says, *We're on our way.*

I breathe a sigh of relief before having it sucked away when my eyes flick from one set of monsters to the other. I'm not sure which one to go to first. In the corner of my eye, a flash of brown runs past—Fenrir charges straight toward Jormungandr. Snarling, the hound runs at the serpent from behind, his feet pounding against the hard surface of Asgard. His teeth bite into the serpent's flesh. He rips out a portion of the Midgard serpent's side, and Jormungandr rises up and hisses, flicking his body from side to side. The thrashing knocks Fenrir away. He's sent flying and lands in a heap on the ground with a yelp.

After a quick glance in Fenrir's direction, the Midgard serpent continues to attack Thor. The god of thunder spins and releases his hammer, hitting the Midgard serpent in the side with a wallop, distracting the serpent from Fenrir. Thor seems to have already pieced together that the hound is on our side. Fenrir pushes himself up with difficulty, but his determination sets in. He rises to his feet and heads back to attack his brother again.

"I'm not letting you bully me anymore," Fenrir growls to the serpent. "You did that enough when I was a pup, and you were mean and nasty. Even Hel agrees with me."

If Jormungandr can understand him or hear him, I do not know. He doesn't respond to Fenrir's words. This doesn't discourage Fenrir, who charges forward and takes another bite at the serpent's side. After a loud hiss, the serpent again flicks his body, aiming toward Fenrir, but this time, Fenrir is ready. He springs to the side, an agile hound even for his size. The serpent twists, aiming for the hound with his head, and Thor whacks Jormungandr from the other side with his hammer then summons lightning to hit on the other side of the serpent. When the serpent flicks around to head toward Thor, I throw stinging magic, hitting Jormungandr on his nose. Each time, the serpent hisses with a different type of attack, yet he doesn't give up. He's determined to get to that palace and kill Thor.

After watching the commotion, I decide to remain with the group fending off the Midgard serpent. Currently, fewer are fighting the serpent. Either way, it doesn't matter which enemy I attack. We are still outnumbered, and we need the help of the dragons. We could really use the help of other realms also.

As I join the group fending off the serpent, another roar sounds in the distance. Turning, I spot Drogon firing a plume of flame at one of the lava monsters, a big gash running down his side.

On the ground, the draugar are almost at us, heading toward the serpent area as though they're about to attack Thor, Fenrir, Loki, and me. Suddenly, I realize I can't see Loki. How predictable. Once again, the god of mischief isn't around to help. He's probably betrayed us. Right then, I promise that if I get out of this alive, I will never trust him again.

Chapter Seven

The rainbow colors of Bifrost illuminate across the sky, and moments later, a shifting cloud of dark-winged angels of death heads our way. Between a couple, they carry the beautiful goddess Freya and place her down gently beside me before taking off and attacking the draugar. Another couple of angels of death lower a familiar figure to the ground next to the goddess.

As I step away from the fighting, a flood of relief washes over me. Not only did the angels of death come, but they also brought Beowulf. The angels of death release Midgard's monster slayer on the ground near us and join their brothers fighting off the monsters.

The animal-skin-clad man crosses his forearms and thumps his fists against his bare chest. "Beowulf, at your service!"

My mouth quirks at his primitive salute. "Thank

you for coming, Beowulf. We could use your help." My greeting is heartfelt. Though the man wanted to kill our dragons the first time he saw them, he has grown on me, and he has proven his ability to fight the monsters. "Take a pick which monsters you would like to fight." I indicate the three different kinds, and his eyes light up seeing the lava monsters.

He points to the moving giant lava pits. "I always wanted to fight one of them before. I didn't get a chance when I went to Muspelheim to help get you. Instead, we resorted to sneaking out of the realm. Very disappointing!"

I nod, and without a second glance, he sprints to the other side of the battlefield, his spear held high.

Freya strolls sensuously toward me, the fabric of her long skirt swaying with her hips. The bodice of her dress clings to her torso, leaving little of her curves to the imagination. A smile crosses her kind face, the expression deceptive over her ability to lead a war. If I hadn't seen her command her soldiers, the angels of death, into combat, I would doubt she should be here.

The goddess eyes Jormungandr cautiously, ensuring she stands a considerable distance from the serpent. She then observes her warriors as they fight the draugar before surveying the lava monsters in the background. The winged Valkyries and the few dragons have barely slowed the lava monsters. We need the aid of the dragons from the wasteland and the rest of Odin's armies.

"Thank you for coming, Freya," I say again when her eyes return to me. "Thank you for bringing your warriors."

Freya smiles warmly. "Of course we came. It's important that Asgard stays strong and that Ragnarok doesn't happen. Your problem here is much bigger than the current warrior count can combat successfully. Where are all the other realms and their armies to help? Have you rallied any other armies or the other realms?"

I rub my upper arm. "Odin is supposed to be rallying the gods and einherjar. Elan is seeking aid from the dragons of the wasteland. I'm not sure where they are. I thought they would have been here by now." I worry my bottom lip. "As for the other realms, I don't have a way to contact them except through Ratatoskr." I pull a face. "He wouldn't be my first choice, nor a messenger I could trust for something like this. Although I did consider him briefly before I contacted you."

A shooshing of a sword captures my attention, and I spot an angel of death's blade slicing through one of the draugar. I inwardly cheer over the success as the undead falls to the ground. My celebration is cut short when the draugar gathers itself up and hauls itself to its feet to resume attacking. The scene of the battle of the draugar is horrific. Several undead are dissected and have lost limbs yet remain unaffected. They gather up their severed limbs and reattach them before resuming their attacks.

Even though they're fighting over three hundred feet away, the smell is overbearing. The angels of death bear that strange smell of death, and so do the draugar. I'm confident, though, the draugar smell worse.

Freya's face turns pale, and she wrings her hands. "I will contact the different realms. We need more help."

Nodding, I turn back to help Thor with Jormungandr, only to halt seconds later. A dragon wails in the distance, and I spot Naga spinning uncontrollably with Eir on his back. The Valkyrie grabs his reins. Her light-brown ponytail whips wildly around her face. Naga careens closer to the ground, and every muscle in my body seizes, knowing I'm powerless to stop it.

A flash of brown catches my eye, and Drogon dives toward the blue dragon. A streak of red, and Tanda joins him. The two dragons descend past Naga and change direction to shift under the blue dragon. Drogon grabs Naga's back legs, and Tanda takes the front. In a unified motion, they toss the blue dragon away from danger and farther into the air. All the time, Eir is saddled on his back.

After several twists and turns, Naga finally regains control of his flight, and my shoulders melt from relief. A cloud of white wings surrounds the blue dragon as a group of winged Valkyries check on the blue dragon and Eir.

Something red drops to the ground, and Tanda sits on the ground out of the battle ring, her red scaled face drained. I remember the slash she received earlier from the lava monster, and unease twists in my stomach.

Jormungandr lashes at Thor, his fangs catching his pants and scraping his skin. Thor staggers away, blood seeping around the cut in his pants. The serpent has another go at Thor, and the god heads for the nearest boulder, ducking behind its safety. I run after him, jumping out of the way as the serpent charges at me with his fangs spread, ready to mark me with his venom. I shoot a stinging shot at the serpent when he rears, ready to attack me again.

Loki appears out of nowhere and shifts in the middle of the serpent's attack, blocking his monster son with his magic barrier.

Too preoccupied to ponder where the mischievous god appeared from, I sprint behind the boulder with Thor. "Have you been struck by venom?"

Thor's face has lost all color, and his breath is ragged. "I think so. My energy is depleting quickly, and I feel like I want to be sick." His head rolls to the side. "Not only that, every part of my body burns with a hot piercing feeling."

Instantly I use my magic to draw the venom out of my leader's system, vaguely aware of what's happening around me.

Freya rushes behind Loki to get to Thor and aid me with his healing. Jormungandr lashes at us again, attempting to pass over Loki, only to be blocked by his father's barrier.

Loki tuts. "Now, now, son, that's not the way to treat Kara and Freya." He shakes his head with disbelief. "I thought you would have more manners than that."

Jormungandr thrashes against Loki's barrier, his beady eyes angry and determined to break through.

The god manages to hold the barrier firm even when the serpent hisses at him. Loki feigns hurt. "That's not a way to treat your father either."

The Midgard serpent doesn't relent. Loki grunts, and I see he is running out of energy. His barrier is fading. Even a god with magic as strong as Loki's struggles against this enormous creature.

Intelligent enough to know a magic barrier blocks his way, Jormungandr swerves around to the side, and Loki has to put up another barrier to block that direction. The serpent darts to the other side. Loki shifts the barrier in the middle to block the other side. The god's energy wavers more, and I feel for him, having been there many times before. His brow is wet with perspiration, and he wipes it on his shoulder, careful to not break his barrier.

Loki looks up at his son. "I thought you were supposed to be upset because I was captured?"

The serpent remains unresponsive other than continuing to work around the barriers. Fenrir attacks his brother from the side, only to be flicked away by the serpent's enormous body. He yelps when he crashes into a boulder and struggles to get to his feet.

Thor groans, and I look back down at him and continue to help Freya drain out the venom. Slowly, the black poison is drawn out of the puncture marks in his calf.

My leader lays his head back against the boulder. "I'm so exhausted."

I clasp his upper arm. "Hang on, Thor. You can't let go. We need you to help battle these monsters."

"I don't know if I can." Thor's voice is raspy.

"You're going to have to. You can't give up to the

Midgard serpent this early, or else the serpent will take this realm." I grip his arm tighter.

My attention is drawn away by the slicing of swords, and I glance over quickly to see how the battle is faring. The angels of death are still fighting the draugar. My hopes waver when I realize they aren't getting anywhere, especially when the undead simply gather their limbs, attach them back to their bodies, and continue their attack.

The other Valkyries continue to battle the lava monsters, with Drogon and Hildr casting barriers to block as many attacks as possible. Still, with Hildr the only one wielding the magic, it's impossible to stop the lava monster's attack. It took all four of us on Helheim to hold back the monsters. I search for Naga and Tanda and spot them on the side of the battlefield, their dragon bodies sprawled across the ground. Eir hovers over Naga and Britta over Tanda; the two Valkyries are attempting to heal their friends. After trying to heal Elan when she was poisoned by the monster, I know their efforts won't be enough.

The winged Valkyries attempt to use different attacks they have been taught, each one gaining little purchase against the giant walking lava pits. I watch as more of their swords melt inside the lava cracks. They aren't going to be able to hold off the lava monsters for long. A grunt from Loki as he struggles to hold off the Midgard serpent with his magic barrier draws me back to my own area. My hands are still over Thor's wound on his leg as small amounts of venom seep out of his wound. "Come on, Thor. You can heal. Let's get you back on your feet." My energy is also draining after the effort to draw the venom out of his veins.

Thor's eyes close. "I don't know if I can. I just want to roll over and go to sleep."

Chapter Eight

There's no sleeping on the job, little god.

Eyes wide, I spin around, searching for my beautiful dragon. Elan turns visible, her large body towering over me. Her golden eyes meet mine, instantly washing me with a sense of peace.

"Elan!" I cry. "I'm so glad to see you!"

She nudges me with her nose, and I wrap my arms around her snout, allowing myself this moment of happiness. Cries of war in the distance and the hisses of the Midgard serpent pull me back to reality, and I search for the other dragons.

I don't see a single dragon in sight other than our four friends already here. "Are they coming?"

Of course they are. They're just over there. Elan indicates with her nose, and I follow the direction to see a large swarm of dragons coming this way. Relief washes over me, nearly knocking me to my knees, then I spot the gods and einherjar marching toward us from the direction of the palace.

Freya crouches over Thor and continues to heal him as Loki holds the barrier in place to protect them. Loki's face is pale, and his knees start to shake, but he doesn't give up. Fenrir sinks his teeth into the serpent's side again, tearing out a piece of flesh and flicking it to the side. The brown hound lurches to tear out another piece, taking longer to pull away the more significant chunk.

Elan peers down at Thor and nudges him with a talon. *Come on, sleepy god. Get up!*

Thor whines, and his head lolls to the side. "Careful, eating companion. I'm sore."

Boohoo, come on! You can't sleep on the job. Elan nudges him harder with her nose.

He groans and slowly rolls to his hands and knees.

Elan shakes her head. *Unbelievable! I thought you were made of tougher stuff than this,* she chides, yet her eyes are full of concern. Elan picks my leader up in her talons and gently places him on his feet.

Color returns to Thor's cheeks as he stumbles then leans against the boulder, right before Odin directs the gods to the area.

Odin eyes his son, a moment of concern passing

through his one eye. "Do you have it under control here?"

Thor nods once, still loafing against the boulder, his arm resting against his stomach. Thor's eyes are almost pleading for confirmation as he studies Elan while talking to his father. "The dragons are coming, and they're going to help us with Jormungandr."

Elan nods. *That's correct. Most of them will help with the serpent.*

Odin stands straight, his burgundy cape swooshing around his legs, and taps Gungnir against the ground. "Right! Then we shall fight against the lava monsters."

"Or the draugar," Freya adds, her concerned eyes watching her angels of death struggle against the undead.

Thor pushes off the boulder. "I think that is the best option."

Something catches Odin's eye, and he turns, halting on the spot when he sees Loki free. Odin eyes his blood brother with distrust, his hand twitching over his sword. Then he pauses as he seems to realize the god of mischief is working against Jormungandr. Thrusting an arm toward the monsters in the distance, Odin commands, "Gods, let us unite and fight these obscene creatures."

With swords raised, many gods and warriors charge toward the monsters, expelling a unified war cry.

"Tyr?" A flash of brown bolts past us, running up to the god of war.

Tyr turns just in time to see Fenrir charge up to him, and he wraps his one arm around the hound's snout in a hug. "Fenrir! It's so good to see you free and happy again." The god roughs up the fur on the hound's snout, and Fenrir rubs his head affectionately against Tyr's armor.

Jormungandr strikes at the hound, and Tyr pulls him out of the way before drawing his sword and stabbing at the serpent's nose. Pulling back with a hiss, the serpent redirects and strikes at a couple of straggling gods as they pass.

Fenrir nudges Tyr's side. "Thanks. But I got this. It's great to see you again, but they need you elsewhere, especially now that the dragons have arrived." His big brown eyes turn soft. "It is great to see you again."

"It's good to see you too. We'll catch up after the battle." Tyr rubs him one last time behind an ear before joining a couple of other gods to fight the draugar.

The first round of dragons arrive, and they dig

their talons into Jormungandr, taking his attention away from the gods.

Odin eyes Thor, skepticism leaching out of his one eye, before he turns to join the other gods. Fenrir lunges at Odin from behind a boulder. Odin swivels, and Fenrir's teeth rip into his pants and scrape down Odin's thigh. Odin limps quickly away, at the same time swinging his spear at Fenrir as he attacks again. Gungnir's handle hits Fenrir across the jaw, and the hound flinches back before steeling himself and lunging at Odin again. Odin's hurried limp isn't quick enough to take him safely away from Fenrir's next attack, and his face pales knowingly. I ready myself to step in between the hound and the god, but Loki beats me to it.

The mischievous god shifts between them to block his hound son's next attack and raises his hand in a stopping motion. His chest heaves with exhaustion. "I know he deserves it, Fenrir. But we have bigger fights to battle today. Let it rest."

His eyes fixed on Odin, Fenrir's top lip curls, exposing a few of his enormous canine teeth. The hound lowers his gaze to his father. "As much as I respect your wishes, Father, I don't think I should."

Loki casts Fenrir a weary smile. "And I respect your wishes too, Fenrir. But maybe it's best if you leave it for today."

Fenrir growls as he eyes Odin. "We'll see."

Elan shifts, standing behind Loki to become another barrier between Odin and Fenrir.

Jormungandr strikes at Fenrir, his fangs narrowly missing the hound. Fenrir yelps as he's knocked off his feet and lands on his side. The hound scrambles to his feet, ready to attack his brother.

I charge to Odin and set to work healing him. My exhaustion is already prominent, and I wonder how I will make it through this battle. I must recharge soon. As soon as the god is healed enough to move freely, Odin rises and joins the other gods.

The next wave of the dragons joins the battle. Thor clasps his belt of strength then throws Mjollnir at the serpent. The wallop is followed by a hiss from Jormungandr. The sound increases into a high-pitched protest as the dragons tear into the serpent's flesh. While checking on my friends in the distance, I see more glowing red eyes peer out of the darkness of Yggdrasil's trunk. This time as they climb over the top of the hole's lip, it's hellhounds that add to the collection of monsters.

Eingana lands next to me, watching over her daughter and the other dragons as they attack the serpent. She is larger than her daughter, and many of her features are the same as Elan's, yet as the mother dragon peers down at me, the wisdom in those eyes fills me with awe. This dragon still mesmerizes me.

I blink and attempt to concentrate. The first time I saw this dragon, I didn't know she was the leader of the dragons. I had stood in the middle of her nest with Elan's egg clutched in my hand. Reluctantly, she had spared me because I had saved her clutch from the zmey. It was the best move I've made in my life. "Thank you for coming, Eingana. We appreciate your help and the help of the dragons."

Of course I would come, Kara, and bring all the dragons from the wasteland. We want Asgard to be safe as well. It's our home too. Her eyes travel from her daughter to Odin, disappearing in the distance. *I see my daughter has grown wise with your influence.*

I almost choke on my saliva. "I don't think it's my influence. I think she's reflecting your leadership and slowly maturing and taking on more responsibilities."

Amusement flickers through her golden eyes. *Young Valkyrie, you're too modest. Your influence on my daughter has been tremendous, and it all started when you saved her life before she hatched. You have also helped raise her to be a mature and natural leader. I have always been thankful for your pairing.*

The leader of the dragons straightens her back, reminding me Elan still has some growing to do before she is full size. Eingana scans the grounds, her eyes turning serious as she assesses the situation. *We must fight. This is not acceptable.*

The air of authority surrounding Eingana deepens. From the first moment I met her, Eingana was authoritative and a force to be reckoned with, her hate for our kind unwavering. That changed after I bonded with her daughter. Simply knowing her has brought so much meaning to my life.

Curious gargling noises come from the draugar, distracting me in time to catch Freya heading toward her warriors fighting the undead.

Hearing a strange groan behind me, I find Thor clasping his hammer and his belt of strength. He staggers forward to an open patch near the Midgard serpent and holds Mjollnir high, summoning lightning. Several dragons surround the serpent in the sky and on the ground. Dread pours into me. "Wait, Thor! You don't want to hit the dragons."

Thor's shoulders sag with defeated understanding, and he lowers his hammer to his side. He's always been careful about this in the past. His eyes are bleak as he looks at me and nods. "You're right." He staggers a few more feet forward and presses his back against the nearest boulder. "I don't know why I didn't think of that. Jormungandr's venom must have affected my brain."

He's still weak, and I wonder whether he's ready to fight. The screams of war fill my ears from behind, and I notice Thor's face turn pale, causing my panic to escalate. Maybe he's questioning his own ability to keep going.

Chapter Nine

Jormungandr is surprisingly agile on land. He proceeds very quickly and smoothly, far different than I pictured the movement of a monster with that enormous weight and no legs.

Determined not to hit the dragons, Thor checks the path is clear before he spins and releases his hammer at the Midgard serpent. He seems to have gathered his resolve, pushing away all signs of lethargy and effects from the venom. Mjollnir slams into Jormungandr, causing him to hiss with frustration and pain. Then the dragons attack him from all sides, intensifying the serpent's protests.

The Midgard serpent thrashes then springs at different dragons, mouth open, ready to strike. He rears, only to be bitten from behind by another dragon. Jormungandr hisses and coils back, mouth remaining open and threatening.

Dredging up my remaining energy, I do my best

to block the serpent with magic and attack him with stinging blows. Each attack on the serpent seems to lose intensity. After being struck and torn so often, the serpent appears to be building immunity to pain, especially strikes by my magic. The lack of effect renders me almost useless, and I hate the feeling of helplessness as he lunges at the nearest dragon. Jormungandr clasps a red dragon within his jaws, clamping down and expelling loud cracks as the bones of the dragon break. The serpent shakes his head vigorously and flings the dragon off to the side. The red dragon falls lifeless to the ground a few feet away from a small group of dragons. My own sadness is reflected in the dragons' faces, and it takes me a moment to steel my reserve before I draw my sword to continue to fight.

Many dragons attack Jormungandr from the other side with added ferocity after losing of one of their own. The serpent lunges at another dragon, narrowly missing a smaller blue dragon that is so much like Naga. Inwardly, I cheer for the little blue dragon's escape. A golden dragon swoops above the spot vacated by the blue dragon and drags his talons along the serpent's head.

Elan tenses beside me. *Careful, Sobek.*

Those two words escalate my tension. I don't want any of Elan's immediate family to get hurt. My heart settles when her brother flies out of the serpent's reach.

Elan fights by my side, protecting me from certain blows, pushing me out of the road, and attacking the serpent with her impressive teeth, ripping shreds from the monster's skin. In my peripheral vision, I see Vanir gods exiting the World Tree, weapons in hand. A small taste of relief covers my tongue. They are our closest neighbors. Freya must have managed to contact someone to spread the word to help. The gods begin with the hell-hounds, some spreading and starting on the lava monsters. It's good to see other realms joining the fight to save our realms.

Loki stands beside me right as a movement catches my eye in the World Tree, and a flash of red moves around the branches.

Squinting, I ask, "Is that Ratatoskr?"

The tiny flash of red is impossible for me to distinguish from this distance. It's only the color and speed that leads me to conclude it's the squirrel.

Loki's pointed nose distorts as he squints in the direction I point. "Looks that way."

"Did he bring the Vanir, or did Freya?" I ask.

Loki shrugs. "You must admit it's a bit surprising that the squirrel would spread the word to bring peace."

I nod. "True. I thought the rodent would've taken pleasure in this chaos."

"You have a point." Loki charges to the side and places a barrier stopping the Midgard serpent from attacking a group of dragons.

He receives a scowl for his effort.

We don't need your help, egg stealer, a brown multi-horned dragon snarls at the god.

Loki raises his hands in defeat and backs away. "Only trying to make amends for my actions."

The brown dragon exposes his extensive array of teeth. It looks as though Loki has a long way to go before he's forgiven for the times he stole their eggs. I don't really blame them. The god is too untrustworthy. It's impossible to know exactly what he's planning and who will benefit from his actions other than himself.

The mischievous god glances over at the lava monsters below, and I follow his gaze. All feeling vanishes from my cheeks. Emerging from Yggdrasil's trunk, Hel holds her hands high, conjuring magic, followed onto the realm by more monsters. I don't know where she's gathered them from, and I wonder if there's more on Helheim that she can command to attack us.

"This isn't good." His face wan, Loki tugs at his black leather sleeve. "Maybe I can reason with her like I did with Fenrir. Unlike the serpent, she is the mature one who thinks things through. Jormungandr seems to have his own agenda, different from the other children."

He turns to leave, and I follow him. "I'm coming with you."

"You don't have to," Loki says.

I quicken my pace to walk next to him. "We can't trust you yet. You haven't proven yourself, so I'm coming with you. As far as I know, you could be colluding with Hel and ready to bring down Asgard in one final sweep."

Loki frowns. "Oh, Kara. I'm hurt. I thought you would trust me by now. I've done nothing but do the best for you and protect you."

Sword tip facing the ground, I cross my arms. "You can keep telling yourself that, but I don't believe it."

Chapter Ten

More monsters and draugar follow Hel out of the tree trunk, and Loki leads me through the battles and warriors, avoiding the most dangerous situations. Ominous darkness emerges from the World Tree, clouding the area surrounding Hel and the lava monsters. Hel waves her arms dramatically, conducting the shrouds of mist and darkness she has brought with her from the under realms. As if the invasion of darkness overwhelming Asgard's bright sky wasn't threatening enough, more draugar and lava monsters climb out of the trunk of Yggdrasil.

As he approaches from the other end of the battlefield, the track Loki weaves toward Hel is obscured by many draugar and lava monsters. Staying close by his side, we fight our way together, Loki using his advanced magic while I use a combination of magic and weaponry.

A draugar comes at me, and Loki darts in front and blocks it with a magic shield. Deep concentration lines cross his pale pointed face as he embraces the monster with his magic before the undead explodes in front of us. My jaw drops with disbelief as he continues to defend me. Confusion clouds my mind, coupled with the shock that we can do that with our magic.

Another draugar comes from the other side, and Loki shoots magic from his hand, knocking it backward. A weird sound comes from behind me, and I turn to be confronted with a draugar only two feet away. Swiping my sword, I narrowly miss then finish by jabbing the blade straight into the monster's heart. The eerie creature keeps coming. I stumble backward, drawing the sword out of its body, and it comes at me again. The lack of living organs and the ability to reconstruct themselves makes them hard to beat.

Loki thrusts his hand at the undead coming for me, and the monster is flung backward when hit by a bolt of magic. "You should be hitting these with magic, not with swords. Your sword will be useless unless you cut off its head."

Another draugar comes my way, and Loki suddenly appears next to me, distracting it. The mischievous god lures it away, and when the draugar is upon him, he changes into an insect, flies behind the monster, and changes back before exploding it with magic. Pieces of dead flesh and bone plop to the ground around us. Disgusted, I wipe some off my face.

Our path is littered with the undead and the strange, strangled sounds they make. At times, cutting through them is nearly impossible. Adding to the sounds of the draugar, war cries of all kinds reverberate around us. From behind, we're chased by hisses from Jormungandr and roars of pain and frustration from the dragons. I see several dragons have fallen when I gaze behind me, causing me to stress over our friends. I'm not sure where Elan is. I hope she's keeping out of harm's way. Although she should be safe while cloaked in invisibility, unless she lands in the wrong position at the wrong time. I gaze at the sky, looking for her.

I'm right above you, Kara. Hearing my beautiful dragon instantly fills my heart with happiness. *I won't be far away.*

I search the sky again, hoping to catch a glimpse of her even though she's invisible, before slicing off another draugar's head. I pant. *I'm glad you're okay. I can hear all those dragons being hurt, and it's worrying me,* I say through our bond.

Many are getting hurt everywhere. Elan's voice is

full of warmth and understanding. *Including the lava monsters and the serpent. What you hear from the dragons is only a tiny portion. The winged Valkyries and gods are being injured much more.* She pauses, and I feel her mind whirling with thought. *This is war. It's devastating, but it's going to happen.*

The knowledge saddens me. *I know, but I still stress over my friends, and I don't know what I'd do if something happened to you.*

A strange sound captures my attention on my left, and I glance over to see three undead heading toward me. I ready myself to defend, knowing Loki is facing the other direction, when a plume of fire abruptly shoots down and engulfs them, setting their decaying flesh on fire. The stench is horrible, and I want to retch, but I force it down. *Thank you, Elan.*

You never have to thank me. It's my instinct. I will protect you no matter what. Like you, I don't know what I would do if you were hurt or if I didn't have you.

More strange sounds catch my attention on my right. Turning, I shoot magic at the draugar, spotting another one coming my way and Loki battling a draugar farther on my right.

"So much for Hel being upset I was captured," Loki calls over his shoulder as he obliterates another rotten-fleshed monster.

"I know what you mean. If Hel operated these,

you would think they would leave you alone because clearly, you're not a prisoner. Or they simply don't have a brain."

"I'm pretty sure none of them would have a brain," Loki says. "They've been dead, preserved in Hel's magic, for who knows how long. Surely their brains can't function anymore."

Cries of pain from the angels of death and gods surround us, combined with more cries from Valkyries and the roars of dragons and lava monsters. The sound of war is devastating enough without the howls and growls of the monsters around us.

Dark clouds gather farther ahead as more monsters and draugar fold out of the World Tree, Vanir gods knocked down in their path. The bodies lining the sides of the battle are devastating. I feel for each of them, selfishly hoping none of them are people I know.

We are farther through the draugar, heading toward Hel and her many minions climbing out of Yggdrasil. Something red dives from the branches of the World Tree. It takes me a moment to focus and realize Ratatoskr is diving out of the branches with a tiny dagger in hand. The move is almost comical, yet he is determined. He lands on the shoulders of the newest draugar and cuts off its ear. Watching the body piece fall to the ground, the squirrel cries out with satisfaction. The messenger's celebration is short-lived when the draugar continues as though nothing has happened. Undeterred, Ratatoskr stands on his hind legs and pounces at the draugar's arm, cutting at the flesh. When the undead still doesn't respond, the squirrel springs again and runs the dagger across the draugar's throat. It's strangely warming to see the squirrel trying hard to fight the invaders.

My attention is pulled away when several undead approach me. I ready myself to fight them with magic when they are suddenly lifted into the air and thrown to the side. A strange peace fills me, knowing Elan is watching over me and attacking from above.

How many of these horrible creatures is Hel bringing to Asgard? Elan asks. *This is ridiculous! They seem to be never-ending. It's like she's been saving these up for years.*

Perhaps, I say. *Not only that, how many lava monsters does she have from Muspelheim? They also seem never-ending.* I gaze at the World Tree to see other hideous monsters coming out that I've never seen before. Hounds similar to Garm, yet more ferocious, prance onto the realm, ripping into anybody nearby. A flash of brown sprints past me as Fenrir heads straight to Hel as if running to greet his long-lost sister.

Dread fills my stomach with a sickening sludge

before it twists into knots, worrying he will team up with Hel. She has enough monsters on her side.

Fenrir approaches one of the hounds and snarls, snapping his jaws before egging the hellhound into another fight. Loki's son takes one of them down, dodging another before running straight to Hel.

An uneven smile spreads across Hel's face as he stops in front of her, and she pets Fenrir on the head. It's the first time in many years that I've seen the hound's tail wag with happiness for someone other than Tyr. Within moments, he appears to have returned to being the happy pup.

I hurry to catch up with Loki. "He's not going to join Hel, is he?"

Loki blasts another draugar with exploding magic and knocks more undead several feet off to the side. "I don't know what he's going to do." Annoyance laces Loki's voice. "He's kind of been loyal to me, but I believe he and Hel had a good bond when they lived together in Jotunheim."

Fenrir presses his head against Hel's stomach, and she hugs him around the neck. The simple, unreserved show of affection has me stressed, sending my heart thumping profusely. We don't need Fenrir to fight with Hel. We have enough to deal with now. Approaching closer, while fighting off the draugar, we reach the area attacked by lava monsters. Large rock-covered arms swing through the air, knocking down several gods fighting at its feet. Beowulf charges at a monster, spear poised, expelling a loud battle cry, and tosses it into the lava monster's head. A look of satisfaction plasters over his face, only to be washed away a moment later when the spear shaft bursts into flames. The monster slayer quickly searches the surrounding area for discarded weapons and finds another spear. He dodges the lava monster's arm as it swipes at him, then throws the newfound spear at the monster's leg before searching for another discarded weapon. His fighting skills are impressive, considering he is human without the benefit of added strength, size, magic weapons, or magic.

Loki and I dodge around the monsters as they fight the dragons, Valkyries, and gods. We steer wide of the next giant monsters. Our first goal is to approach Hel. Maybe Loki can reason with his daughter and stop this war.

Another lava monster sweeps its large arm over the top of us, and we duck, even though it was probably too high to catch us.

Jeez! that was close. Elan's voice fills my head.

I look up, even though I know she's probably still invisible. *Did that nearly get you?*

Yes. It just missed me. I didn't see that one coming.

Then rise higher, Elan, even if they can't see you. I don't want you hurt.

Elan sighs. *I'm not going much higher. You need all the help you can get.*

At least go high enough so you're out of danger, I plead.

Another whoosh sounds above me, and I duck as the lava monster's hand glides over the top of me. There's no noise from Elan.

Did that miss you, Elan? I ask when the silence grows too much.

Yes, I'm fine. I'm above the lava monster. She sounds as though she is puffed.

We approach Fenrir and Hel, with Loki leading the way. Hel's arms remain locked around the hound's neck, and his happy, wagging tail doesn't waver. A niggling worry turns in my stomach. I'm convinced Fenrir will join her.

Chapter Eleven

"Fenrir, my dear son." Loki opens his arms wide, ducking slightly to avoid another swipe from a lava monster. "What are you doing?" He side-steps a hellhound and seems unfazed as he's followed by the glowing red eyes.

Hel releases Fenrir, observing her father with her uneven face.

Fenrir adjusts his stance to look at his father. "I'm greeting my sister. Hel looked after me when we were alone in Jotunheim. Unlike Jormungandr, she treated me with respect—not like some monster or someone to attack."

Loki chuckles and sounds genuinely pleased. "That's fantastic! I'm so glad you two got along."

Hel studies Loki with an unnerving interest. For the time being, the monsters surrounding us leave us alone as we converse with Hel, as though Hel is directly instructing them. We aren't so lucky with the background chorus comprised of plumes of fire and screams of pain that continues to torture my soul. The sounds are impossible to block out.

Loki tilts his head to one side, his smile spreading wide. "Hel, it's lovely to see you again." His face seems paler than usual, and his shoulder-length black strands sway with the breeze conjured by a giant's swipe nearby.

Hel stands tall and nods curtly to Loki. "Father." There's no emotion in her voice.

"My dear daughter," Loki says. "What are you doing here with all your minions?"

Hel's fleshy eye narrows. "Can't I visit other realms?"

"Of course you can." Loki's upbeat voice remains smooth. "You can visit any realm you like. I was merely wondering why you are bringing all your minions and causing havoc on Asgard." Loki shifts closer then stops when Hel plants him with a look. He smiles broadly as though trying to take away her tension. "I'm confused. You see, I heard all three of you were upset because I was captured."

He rocks on his toes and clasps his hands behind his back. "As you can see, I am no longer captured, so there's no reason for all this kerfuffle." The god keeps his voice light-hearted as he waves his arms toward the chaos in the background.

Hel's almost-black eyes scan the background and the commotion of war behind us, eventually landing on me. She trains a scolding look on Loki. "What gave you the impression your capture upset me?"

Loki shrugs. "That's what I was told. I was told you children were so upset I was captured, and your love for me has caused you to lash out at Asgard." Pride fills his face, finished with a grin. "I must admit, I can't blame you. I would be quite upset too."

Hel raises her fleshy eyebrow. "Well, whoever told you that was wrong."

Loki's jaw drops, and for once, he is lost for words. "But…"

"You were never a father to us. You left us alone in a cave under our mother's guidance." Arms on hips, Hel moves closer to him, her height dwarfing his, and she scowls. "We were left to fend for ourselves, and I don't even remember you coming to visit. Our mother didn't care for us either because we were monsters and not her species. Still, she occasionally visited us and made sure we had shelter and the bare minimum food supply." The goddess straightens her back, tilting her head to peer down at Loki, showing off some of her inherited height from her giant mother. "So what makes you think we care that you were locked up or held by the Asgardians?"

Loki's unease grows under her gaze, and he backs

away a few steps. His attempt to keep peace with a grin is all teeth and no sincerity. "Fenrir seemed to care."

Fenrir nods, but his eyes bear confusion as his gaze travels from Hel to his father.

Hel affectionately places a hand on top of Fenrir's head. Her skeletal hand rubs around his ears, and Fenrir's tongue lolls out to one side as he tilts his head into the scratch. "As much as I love Fenrir and will always protect him when I can, he's not the smartest. However, he is loyal like a hound and is often quick to forgive and be your friend. You have to wrong him entirely to feel his wrath." She gives him a squeeze around his neck, and the hound licks her along the skeletal side of her face.

A frown crosses Loki's face. "But Odin's prophecy—"

"Is a load of rubbish." Hel finishes the sentence for him, dusting the skirt of her black dress with her hands. "The part where we're all going to attack Asgard is correct and is most likely the outcome of Ragnarok. As for us being upset because you are captured—" She huffs. "We couldn't care less." She glances sideways at her hound brother, her mouth in a thin line on one side and all exposed teeth on the other. "Perhaps Fenrir did, but the rest of us didn't. We are simply out to get our own."

"Don't you care for me at all?" The heartbreak and neglect on Loki's face are real.

With a roll of her eyes, Hel says, "He finally realizes." She thrusts a hand toward the god, hitting him with a powerful wall of magic.

Loki flies back and lands on his backside, his pride hurt more than anything else.

Fenrir runs to his father's side, and with his brows knitted in confusion, he gazes back at Hel. "Hey! Don't hurt Father."

The goddess raises her chin. "You are either on my side or your father's. What is it, Fenrir? I hope you won't fight against me after everything we've been through together."

Climbing to his feet, Loki strokes Fenrir's snout. "I also hope you won't fight against me either. I love you, my dear son. I have thought about you daily, and I'm glad you're released from your shackles as I am also released from mine."

Somehow, I don't think Loki's words are true, but I hold back my opinion, especially if it has the potential to help save Asgard.

Sadness and confusion fill Fenrir's face as he looks between his two closest family members, love filling his eyes in equal amounts as he gazes at both. But Hel is making him choose a side. "You're making this decision too hard. I don't want to fight against either of you."

Hel's resolve stiffens. "You must pick a side, Fenrir."

The hound's worry deepens. "But I can't."

Loki places a hand on the hound's shoulder and rubs the spot affectionately. "You don't have to pick a side, Fenrir, just like you don't have to fight. Just don't fight against me. That's all I ask. This time, I'm fighting for Asgard."

Hel's one eyebrow rises. "And why is that?"

Loki thrusts his hands out to the sides. "Because I want somewhere to live. If Asgard is destroyed, then many other realms will also be destroyed. Maybe not Helheim, but everywhere else will be. Don't take it the wrong way, but I don't want to live in darkness for the rest of my life. I would find that rather depressing living without sunshine, constantly shrouded in darkness."

Hel's face seems to be set in stone, and she tilts up her chin. "That's all you deserve." She turns to Fenrir, who remains seated by Loki. "Are you coming to fight with me, Fenrir?"

The fur on Fenrir's face doesn't hide his distress. His big brown eyes are filled with sadness and confusion. He clearly doesn't want to disappoint either his father or his sister. His brown ear stands straight as a loud hiss from Jormungandr catches his attention, and he observes the situation. Another dragon has been struck and falls to the ground. He looks back at Hel. "Will you be upset if I fight against my brother? I won't be fighting against you or against Asgard, but I will be fighting my brother for all the hassles he's given during my life. I wish to get some of my own back."

Hel observes Fenrir then Loki before her black eyes land on Jormungandr. She takes her time assessing the two and pondering her answer.

Chapter Twelve

After a long wait, Hel nods to Fenrir. "I remember all the times he tormented you when you were a pup. I won't be upset if you fight against your brother. I understand, even though you're technically fighting against me because you're protecting Asgard. It's between you and our brother. I doubt I need him to win this battle anyway. I have many more creatures to call on."

Fenrir dashes to Hel and presses his face against her, and she hugs him around his neck again.

She ruffles his ear. "Go and get your revenge. My minions will listen to me and leave you alone. Just stay out of our way."

Fenrir charges toward his brother, dodging all Hel's other monsters and staying away from the hell-hounds ready to snap at him. As Hel promised, the hounds don't chase him. There is joy in Fenrir's posture as he runs toward the serpent.

Hel's eyes narrow on Loki. "As for you and your precious little darling you've given more attention than any of your children." She eyes me. "I am going to send you to your grave. Or perhaps I'll spare you, Father, but I'm going to kill your favorite Valkyrie. She was in Thor's group that insulted me, and I'm owed revenge."

My knees quake as Hel lifts her hands. I know there's no way I'm going to be able to stand against her with all the powers that she holds. She is a goddess and a daughter of Loki, instantly giving her more powerful magic than I will ever have. Hel twirls her arms and raises them high. She cups her magic and sends it toward me.

Something yanks me off the ground and into the air. *Grab your cloak, and let's turn invisible.* Soft comfort envelops me with Elan's voice. She flings me up into the air then catches me on her back, swerving between lava monsters.

I reach into my saddlebag and pull on my dragon scale coat, turning invisible with Elan.

Elan flies high over the area of the lava monsters, giving me an overall view of the battle. When I see Hildr and Drogon still fighting hard with only a few injuries, relief floods over me. I can't see Naga and Tanda. They are probably still on the ground, being tended to by their bonded

Valkyries. They could really do with Gilroma's help.

Elan circles, and I gaze back at Loki to see him on the ground with Hel towering over him. The displeasure on her face is evident even from here.

Using my mind speak, I ask Elan, *Should we grab Loki? It seems cruel to leave him to face his daughter alone. I don't think she's going to spare him.*

Are you serious? Her voice rises an octave. *He has betrayed everyone so many times. He deserves whatever he's getting from his daughter.*

I push my mouth to one side. *I agree, but he may be useful for healing any of the wounds caused by these lava monsters and Jormungandr.*

The father-and-daughter team communicate with wild flailing of their arms and short, abrupt movements. Judging by Loki's changed posture, it looks like he's pleading his case, yet it doesn't look hopeful.

Elan moans. *I guess you're right. But I still think we can leave him there a little longer.*

Remember, I say, *he was the one that healed you after the lava monster attack.*

I know. I can see your point, but I still wouldn't mind getting rid of him once and for all. I'll give it a little longer and let him deal with some of his choices.

Elan passes over the lava monster battlefield

again, and I spot an injured blue dragon lying off to the side, a nasty seeping wound distorting his side. A wingless Valkyrie fusses over him, and my worry escalates.

Elan, is that Naga?

She changes direction and descends near the dragon. I thread my hand underneath her scale, connecting to her dragon vision. Naga's head flops on the ground, and Eir leans over the top of him. The peaceful Valkyrie's face is panicked as she works hard to help heal her dragon.

Yes, it is Naga, Elan answers.

Let's go see if we can help.

Elan descends rapidly and lands with a thump a few feet away from Naga.

Quickly, I flip my legs over her saddle and slide down her side. My boots thud on the hard ground, and I race to Naga's side. "How bad is it?"

Tears streak down Eir's face. "I can hardly hear his heartbeat." She chokes on the words and has trouble swallowing her grief. She inserts magic through her hands gently around the large wound that zigzags between his tough scales. "I've been trying to release the poison from his body, but I'm not getting anywhere. He's so weak." She wipes her face on her sleeve.

Flashbacks of when Elan was sick from the poison

rush through my head, and I can't help but glance at Elan's newly visible form. Concern laces her golden eyes as though she remembers the struggle. She was so weak and crumpled on the ground, unable to move or do anything. I couldn't heal her, no matter how much I tried. Since then, our magic has grown, but I'm not sure it'll be enough.

I kneel next to Eir and shove my hands under Naga's scales, injecting healing magic into his soft skin underneath.

Eir touches his nose, her palm flat against the skin, and she feels for breath. "I can hardly see him breathing. His ribs aren't rising, and his nose isn't expelling any warm air. I'm worried I'm going to lose him." Her tears increase, and she sobs. "What am I going to do?"

I look at her in earnest. "We're going to work as fast as possible to get him the best help. I'll give you a hand to try to draw out the poison. If it doesn't work, we'll find something else." Somehow, I manage to sound encouraging despite struggling with my own emotions.

I continue injecting the healing magic into the dragon, and I attempt the best I can to draw out the poison from the cuts. After being at it for a while, my energy wanes, and I cry, "Come on, Naga. You can do it. Help us pull you back to the land of the living."

Elan nudges him with her nose, and he doesn't respond. *Dragon scales! Is this how bad I was?*

I nod. *That's why I had to get Loki out of his imprisonment. I couldn't let you die. I had to find a way to heal you, and he was the only way I could think of. The only one with magic powerful enough to help you.* I straighten my back. "We should grab Loki," I say out loud.

"Why?" Eir asks, not having heard our conversation through our bond.

"Loki was the one that helped Elan when she was really sick. Remember? That's why he ended up escaping the cave in the first place. It wasn't my intention, but Loki took advantage of it. Thanks to Loki backstabbing me, that's the reason I was placed in Odin's bad books. He robbed me of Odin's trust."

"That makes sense," Eir says, her brow deeply furrowed. "Do you know where Loki is?"

I nod.

"Then go get him," she says.

I jump to my feet, pulling my hand out from underneath Naga's scales before stopping. "Actually, Elan should be able to grab him without me." I gaze at Elan, and she nods. I move back into position and set to work on trying to heal some of Naga's wounds. A gush of wind sweeps around us as Elan's invisible form pushes into the air.

Chapter Thirteen

S hortly after Elan leaves, a stunned Loki is unceremoniously plonked on the ground not far from us.

Elan turns visible. *You were right. He needed saving from his daughter.*

The god's cheeks color. "Let's just say my daughter is a force to contend with. I wouldn't like to be her enemy, although it appears as though I already am."

I stare at him. "Ah. Didn't you realize that before? Considering Hel is the main cause of destruction and the reason we're all here." Naga groans, and I concentrate on him. "If you're remaining on our side, we need you to start healing."

Loki stretches then approaches the blue dragon. "I'm on your side. Not that it appears like I have a choice."

"I need you to do for Naga what you did for Elan.

You know, like that time you used my pain to escape your true prison." I let my spite sneak through.

Loki's face remains blank as he ignores my barb and kneels beside Naga. "Of course I'll heal your peaceful dragon. I'm fond of all your dragon friends."

You've got a long way before you make up for all those dragon eggs you stole, Elan snarls.

Loki places a hand over Naga's wound. "I'm getting the message. Hopefully, I'll make up for it today." Concentration covers his pointy face. "Yes, he does need the kind of healing I gave Elan."

He rises onto his feet and morphs into Gilroma. His shoulder-length locks disappear and are replaced by a bald tattooed head and chin. His dark eyes glow yellow, and he rubs his hands together. Slowly he circles the blue dragon, running his fingers over Naga's scales. He starts to chant and weave around Naga.

"Why do you need to change into Gilroma first?" I ask.

"When I'm in Gilroma's form, I have the ability to conduct my strongest of magic," Loki says.

"Are you saying that your magic is almost nonexistent when you're in the shape of a fly or insect?" I ask.

Loki shrugs and looks at me sheepishly. "You got

me there. There are certain forms that I don't do magic well in, although I can do magic in most forms."

Gently, Elan nears Naga and touches her nose to his. *I can feel his breathing. It's incredibly light, but he's still in there. Don't give up on him.* Warmth radiates through her golden eyes as she focuses on Eir.

Eir gazes up at Elan, her eyes brimming with tears now edged with hope. Wet rivers are carved through her dirt-stained face. "You have no idea how glad I am to hear that." She wipes her nose on her sleeve. "I honestly couldn't bear to lose him."

Elan eyes me. *I know what you mean.*

Squatting next to Eir, I drape my arm around her shoulder. "I have a battle to fight. Are you going to be okay with Loki healing him? He is a much better healer than us."

Eyes fixed on Naga and lines of worry carved into her face, she nods. "We need to win this. We need to make it worthwhile for all the pain and suffering we've already been through. If Naga doesn't make it —" She chokes on her emotions as a fresh wave of tears runs down her face. "If any of our friends don't make it, we need to make sure it wasn't all for nothing."

After injecting another round of healing magic into Naga's nose, I rub Eir between her shoulder blades with the palm of my hand and touch Naga briefly on the side of his cheek. "Get better, Naga. Keep fighting the poison. I look forward to seeing you soon." Rising to my feet, I head to Elan, lever myself onto her saddle, and check that my dragon scale cloak covers every part of my body and saddle.

I look down at Gilroma. "I'd appreciate it if any more of our friends fall, that you heal them as well."

With a sturdy gaze, Loki says, "I stand by my word. Your friends are my friends too."

Filled with skepticism, I hold my tongue. There is no benefit in arguing with him when I need his help. We take to the sky, and Elan circles the battlefield, searching for our friends. We spot more injured dragons lying off to the side of the battlefield, and sadness envelops me. There aren't any signs of riders, although uneasiness rests over me. "Are any of them Tanda or Drogon?"

Not out of those dragons. The pain in Elan's voice is deep. Because of the Valkyrie connection, she is closer to Tanda, Drogon, and Naga, but every dragon is part of their herd.

The destruction below breaks my heart. It's a shame it has come to this. Despite the added help, we are outnumbered, and yet more monsters file through Yggdrasil's trunk. Hel is keeping her word to destroy Asgard, and even the draugar have slaughtered many of our fighters. Jormungandr has slain many dragons, leaving me wondering how Thor and Fenrir are still alive. Perhaps their experience with the serpent has made them wise to the serpent's attacks. Plus, many of the dragons are protecting Thor. The circle of unmoving dragons around the serpent is testimony to this. I hope they survive their injuries.

The winged Valkyries take to the sky, the battle maidens expelling high-pitched battle cries while flinging swords and fighting. Many angels of death do the same. Instead of the light colors of the Valkyrie, their black wings, black hair, and black clothes bring an element of darkness with them. When I catch sight of the still forms of Valkyries and angels of death on the side of the battle, I'm heartbroken. They, too, were once lively warriors. The devastation is vast and much greater than in the last battle. The previous war was against an army of dragons with their dwarf giant riders. This time, we're fighting much bigger monsters. I wonder if even the giants of Jotunheim would be able to fight the lava monsters. The number of frost giants is few.

We rise and fall to the strokes of Elan's wings, assessing the destruction below us and searching for our friends. Elan circles, facing us back toward the serpent right as another dragon falls. "Where are we going, Elan?"

I'm worried about my mother. She is the leader of the dragons and shouldn't be fighting battles like this. The dragons need her to be there for them on the other side of this loss. She has great responsibility. I want to head back to the Midgard serpent and fight against the vile monster. Hopefully, I can protect my mother. I hope that's okay.

Elan fighting the serpent is the last thing I want, especially when I can see all the dragon bodies surrounding Jormungandr. Yet I can feel her worry and pain, and I know it would kill her if I didn't let her go. Swallowing my own concern, I say, "Of course that's okay. I don't care where we fight, as long as we're making a difference to the outcome. I must admit, it's not looking so good right now. Hopefully, things will change." My thoughts are lost with my concern.

What was that?

Blinking, I search, looking for something out of the ordinary. Coming up empty, I ask, "What was what?"

She growls. *I forget you have bad hearing.*

I frown. "I don't have bad hearing, Elan."

Compared to a dragon, you do. Her neck stiffens, her attention on the ground. *Never mind that. I heard some-*

thing. It sounded like Zildryss, and it didn't sound good. Keep an eye out for him.

"Absolutely!" Leaning slightly to the left, I peer over her side, groaning in frustration when my weak eyes don't see clearly enough to see the small dragon from here. Deciding to use Elan's dragon sight instead, I slip my hand under her scales and tap into her sight. Even though technically we'll be looking at the same thing, I may find something to the side of her vision. Even her peripheral vision is more astute than my sight.

Elan circles the same spot. *He must be around here somewhere. I keep hearing him around this area.* Her eyes zoom in on every little figure that moves. She drops closer to the ground.

Her dragon sight doesn't have the colors of my eyes, and I pull my hand out from under her scales to use my own vision. At this height, I have more of a chance of seeing the lilac scales of the little long-mouthed guardian.

The gods battle feverishly, their swords slicing through the draugar, leaking fresh smells of rotting corpses. I hold my hand over my nose in an attempt to stem the nausea. Fighting with one hand, Tyr proves why he is the god of war, striking each enemy with professionalism and accuracy.

Odin's long burgundy cape flings wildly with

each swing of the sword, his skill as refined as many of the gods beside him. His lack of one eye does not sway his resolve. Many gods gather around him, protecting their leader's back and fighting by his side.

A flicker of lilac catches my attention, and I spot Zildryss's little head poking out of a draugar's fist, his tail out the other end. A tiny squeak reaches my ears now that we are closer to the ground. The little dragon writhes within the undead's hands as the rotting creature stretches his beautiful lilac wings and holds the dragon by the tips.

I gasp. "It looks as though that draugar is going to tear off Zildryss's wings."

Chapter Fourteen

"Over there, Elan. Directly below, between a draugar's hands," I yell, pointing to the spot. She can't see my fingers, but she turns as I pull her reins in that direction.

I see him, she says.

Zildryss's tail flicks wildly, and he recoils his head, eyes wide as he expels panicked squeaks.

"Please tell me I'm wrong and that the draugar is only playing with our friend," I plead.

I'm afraid not. It looks like you said, as though the draugar will rip his wings off. Deep distress fills Elan's voice.

My mind whirrs wildly, trying to think of a way to get Zildryss out of this predicament. I don't want to hit the draugar too hard or in the wrong place and actually cause him to rip off the little dragon's wings.

Elan flies alongside the draugar, and I spot my

opportunity. As I yank my sword out of its sheath on my back, it squeals its anticipation. I fling the sword toward the undead in one swift movement, helping it along with my magic. The sword flips and twirls blade side first, preparing for the impact. The sword slices through both the draugar's outstretched arms at the elbows, and relief floods through me when I see the tiny dragon fall unharmed from the undead's grasp.

The sword lands unceremoniously on the ground, and I call it back to me. Its metal wings expand, turning into supple wings, and bring the sword back to my open hand.

Zildryss takes flight, pumping his tiny wings to escape the next attack. His wings are a lilac blur as he follows the sword back to my hand.

"I think Zildryss wants to catch a ride," I say.

As if I could refuse him, Elan says. *The poor little guy must be exhausted. He's probably buried several monsters and run out of energy. Maybe that's how they captured him.*

I search the surface and notice many heads sticking out of the earth. Their mouths still move, but there is no way they can fight. Several of the buried figures are lava monsters, still spewing lava, their only remaining attack available. Their burial must have taken a lot of effort from the tiny dragon. I'm not surprised he's exhausted. "You're right, Elan. Zildryss has been busy. There are so many buried. It's ridiculous."

The sword lands in my hand, Zildryss still following behind, and Elan turns visible, showing the dragon our exact location. The little dragon lands and runs around my shoulders under my dragon scale hood before cuddling up against my neck. I make sure he is completely covered with the hood, turning the little dragon invisible to the world when Elan activates that gift. He pants frantically, trying to catch his breath. He presses his warm tummy against my skin, showing me what he has been through and seen before exhaustion pulls him into sleep. Zildryss's snores rattle my skin. The volume surprises me, and I'm glad we're in the air so no one can hear him, giving his location away.

"The poor little guy is exhausted. Listen to him," I say.

Elan glides to the left. *Oh, I can hear him from here, all right. I'm not surprised. He's done a lot for his size. He needs the rest.*

We head toward the Midgard serpent. Elan seems to freeze underneath me, and we drop a few inches more than normal between the beats of her wings.

"What is it, Elan?"

Tanda is still on the ground, dealing with the lava

monster poison, just like Naga. She's collapsed on the ground.

"Does she need immediate help? Is someone with her?" I ask.

Elan looks behind us. *She's unmoving, and Britta is fretting over her. I believe she's trying to heal her, but she won't have enough magic, like Eir, and you don't have enough.*

"Then call Loki. Tell him he has to go to Tanda as soon as he's finished with Naga," I say.

Already done.

"Can you hear his response?"

Naga is healed enough to tell me what he said. Apparently, he said, of course, he's going to heal Tanda first. Do we really think that badly of him? Snideness shines thoroughly in her voice.

"Ha. Did you tell him we think that lowly of him?" I ask.

Do I ever hold back?

I smirk, thinking of how Loki would take her response. "I don't believe you do."

There has been a small break from monsters from the under realm entering Asgard. Either Hel is confident she has won or she has run out of minions. Somehow, I doubt the latter. She probably has many other sorts of monsters to call upon.

Elan swerves, covering as much area as possible

to assess the damage beneath. Many warriors of all beings are falling, more than we can afford to win this battle, even with all the lava monsters, hell-hounds, and draugar that Zildryss has buried.

Movement at Yggdrasil catches my eye, and fear courses through me as I imagine the worst. Hel must be bringing in more of her monsters. Instead, I spot what can only be elves from Alfheim, both light and dark, emerging out of the trunk. A strange thump reaches my ears, and I notice a few beings near the tree brace their posture in a ready stance.

"What are they doing?" I ask Elan.

It looks like the ground shook. It's strange, though. Normally, that would mean more lava monsters, but only elves are coming out of the hole.

At the edge of the hole, several elves hold their open hands toward the lower part of the inner trunk.

"It looks like they are holding up a barrier," I say.

The elves push their palms downward in unison. A thump follows soon after.

"That looked like they were pushing something," I say.

Maybe they have been holding off more monsters from entering while they exit the tree.

"Do you think that the thump is them pushing the monsters and causing them to fall down the trunk?" I ask.

Possibly.

"At least we have more help," I say.

We reach the area surrounding the Midgard serpent, and Elan swoops and drags her talons along the serpent's scales before rising out of the serpent's reach. Jormungandr doesn't even hiss at the individual attack. There are so many cuts on his skin that the pain probably blends into one. The serpent lashes out at some dragons on the other side and is rewarded with a wall of fire, as the dragons unite and send plumes of fire at the reptile.

Thor spins and releases his hammer at the serpent, finding a spot not blocked by dragons or warriors. Mjollnir thuds against the serpent's side before returning to Thor's hand. The serpent remains focused on Thor, attacking the dragons only when they become too much of a menace. I spot Eingana, and Elan circles down then lands next to her. The serpent is many times bigger than the dragons, and reality hits hard when we land. The serpent is ridiculously huge, and when he looks at us, my fear takes my breath away. It shouldn't shock me this much since we've pursued him over the realms, but seeing him entirely out of water accentuates his size.

Elan turns visible, and Eingana's eyes widen when she spots her daughter next to her.

Elan, you're okay. The relief is evident in her voice.

She moves away from the fight, and Elan follows her. The leader of the dragons looks at me. *And you are too. That's good.* She catches sight of Zildryss snoring softly on my shoulders under my hood. *The poor little guy. He's worked so hard.*

"He's certainly sleeping it off now," I say, feeling my own weariness taking over my body now that my adrenaline has seeped away. "I think we could all use a nap. I'm exhausted."

I'm sure you could. You two and your friends have been to many realms and must be drained, Eingana says.

How do you think things are going here? Elan looks at the massive serpent with wide eyes. *Are you getting anywhere? He's so big. So much bigger than many of us put together.*

Yes, he is, Eingana says. *But between us all, we should eventually defeat him. One side will certainly collapse with exhaustion before the other. And from what I understand, you've already worn him out a little by fighting him in other realms.*

I don't know about exhausting him, but we have certainly been pursuing him in other realms, Elan says.

Fenrir darts forward and bites at his brother's side, removing a chunk of the serpent's flesh. Jormungandr twirls, his large body swirling around, expelling large droplets of venom from his fangs while waiting for his next victim.

Gravity fills Eingana's golden eyes. *We must be careful because his blood is black. It may also be laced with venom. We don't know if it is poisonous, but we're not going to risk it if we have to. If his blood is poisonous, it will kill us or make us very sick if we get it in our bodies.*

The serpent moves, readying to attack.

I'm going to have to join the fight. Eingana takes to the sky again then swoops down, dragging her talons along the serpent's side.

Chapter Fifteen

Thor, Fenrir, and the dragons continue to attack the Midgard serpent as he writhes farther into Asgard. The serpent's black blood leaves long trails behind him, seeping from the deep gashes along the entirety of his body. The blood exudes a strange odor and smells slightly acidic.

The dragons tear deeper gashes into the serpent's skin, but there is still so much flesh of the Midgard serpent to get through, the gashes seem to only make the serpent sore and upset. They are nothing that will stop the serpent from moving forward. The dragons expel plumes of fire over the top of the serpent, burning long trails, yet the serpent only hisses and continues forward.

Elan and I join the battle. I throw my sword and aim my arrows at the eyes as Elan and the dragons dive and tear into the serpent's flesh. After several rounds of helping the dragons and Thor attack the serpent, I ask Elan, "How do you kill a serpent, Elan? We have been at this for hours, and we personally have been at it for days, trying to attack the serpent and stop him. The wounds we inflict seem to only harm the external flesh and don't affect him enough to stop him. There must be a better way."

Elan stays visible so the other dragons can see her hovering above the serpent. *I've never thought about it. That's a good point. We should think of a way to bring the serpent down instead of only hurting him.*

A dragon flies over us, ruffling my hair. My eyes travel to the other monsters attacking Asgard, and I watch as many fall. Seeing all of this destruction causes me to struggle to keep my heart in check as I try to think of the next best move. The angels of death have given up slicing the draugar's limbs and instead wait until the undead come close enough to slice off their heads. The angels have slashed off their limbs and cut them in half, yet the only thing that seems to stop them is taking off the head.

"Maybe the way that the angels of death stop the draugar has some merit. Perhaps their method is the only way to take down the serpent," I say.

That would make sense, Elan says. *Some of the dragons have already taken off Jormungandr's tail tip, which as expected, has done nothing. That'd be like losing a little finger for you or a talon for us. Removing the eyes would hurt it and possibly slow it down, but I still don't think it'll bring us the desired effect. Besides its heart, which is sunken deep inside of that immense, enormous body, the only thing we can attack is the neck to remove the head.*

"You're right, Elan. It'll have to be the head," I say. "How are we going to do that?"

I will relay the idea to my mother, and she can tell the other dragons. Maybe someone will have an idea how to execute this. It's probably the only way, Elan says.

"It sounds like a plan." I relax my grip on the reins. "Let's hold back until it's all planned and the proper attack is underway. Otherwise, we're just wasting our energy. I don't know about you, but I'm exhausted."

While Elan tells her mother, I watch the other dragons pull back, leaving Thor and Fenrir to strike at the serpent. Thor uses the opportunity to drum up some lightning and shoot it down from the sky, striking the serpent's face. I want to retch from the sickly rancid smell of singed skin.

Oh, that's kind of embarrassing, Elan says.

"What is?" I ask, having watched Thor's display and can't imagine how that would be embarrassing when he managed to strike the serpent's nose.

Mother has told everybody that it was my idea, and

they're all backing the idea and are ready to coordinate our attacks.

I scoff. "What's so embarrassing about that? It was your idea."

It was mainly your idea. I just implemented and assisted it, Elan says.

"Then perhaps you should realize that your mother is building you and your name, ready for when you have to take over the dragons."

Oh, that's not going to be for years yet, Elan retorts.

"What makes you say that?"

Dragons live for a very long time, and my mother still has many years to live.

"I'm glad to hear that. But you never know when an accident will happen," I say.

Elan blows a raspberry. *Don't be ridiculous! Mother is extremely cautious and an excellent fighter. Vicious and always alert.*

"I don't doubt it." I wrap the reins around my hand. "But you just never know. When your time's up, your time's up."

Anyway, Elan says. *Let's move on and focus on attacking the Midgard serpent.*

Jormungandr rears up at all the dragons attacking him and towers over Thor. Fenrir has a go at his brother's lower side to no avail. The serpent hardly acknowledges the attack. The lack of response to his attacks seems to annoy Fenrir further, and he attacks the serpent more while yelling abuses. "This is for what you did to me when we were little." The hound sinks his teeth into the serpent's flesh. Twisting his head, his canines embedded to their roots, he pulls backward before releasing. "This is for all those times that you tormented me." He runs for his serpent brother and takes another bite.

The serpent's beady eyes assess the dragons around him, and he sweeps his tail, heading toward the nearest dragons. The tail collides with a red dragon and flicks it ahead. The dragon careens sideways through the air, walloping against a boulder before flopping to the ground. Seeing the still body of the red dragon on the ground sends spikes of dread through me. That could have been Tanda. I blink away tears. I don't want anyone hurt, but this is war, and I hate it. This is the one part I despise as a Valkyrie. As much as I've been trained and expect the devastation, I still can't get used to it.

An einherjar catches my attention. These warriors are the first reason the Valkyries were trained to gather more dying souls from the battlefield. Looking around, I'm thankful we have collected so many warriors.

The distressed roar of a dragon rings loudly as a brown dragon is flung in the wrong direction. It's hard not to see Drogon's face on that dragon coupled with Hildr on his back. The brown riderless dragon flops to the ground, unmoving.

Zildryss flies off my shoulder and sets to work raising sharp rocks from the ground and jabbing them into the serpent. When the serpent starts to pay more attention to a specific dragon, Zildryss pokes him again, pulling his attention away, often giving the dragon in the serpent's crosshairs a chance to fly away.

Eingana rises, towering over the dragons, drawing the other dragons' attention. The leader of the dragon's eyes meet Elan's, and she nods in acknowledgment. Expelling a roar, Eingana gives the order to attack the Midgard serpent in sequence, making sure she emphasizes the neck. The first dragon in line is yellow, and he drags his talons across the serpent's neck. Then the next dragon copies the move, cutting deeper into the same spot. The process is completed one dragon at a time, focusing on the neck, taking the wounds deeper into the serpent's flesh as other dragons singe the gashes with plumes of fire. The serpent cries out as the cuts grow deeper. The neck is enormous, but there are a lot of dragons, and they continue, getting deeper and deeper, until finally hitting an area deep within his flesh.

The wound weeps, and the attack is slow and cruel, but unless the serpent stops tormenting the realms, he cannot live. Dragon after dragon attacks Jormungandr's neck. Some fly over the top while others attack under the neck. Others on the ground bite out chunks, ripping out mouthfuls and spitting them off to the side. The gash around the neck grows deeper. The serpent continuously moves, making the incision around the neck messy, tearing up more surface flesh than necessary. Despite all of this and the pain the serpent must be in, he continues to move.

Elan pauses her attacks and lands. I climb off and drop to the ground. I throw my sword, and the Midgard serpent spots me. His eyes narrow, and his mouth opens, exposing fangs. He strikes at me quicker than I have time to react.

Chapter Sixteen

Springing into action, I zigzag in the other direction. A rock skitters past me as through joining my race to run away as the serpent narrowly misses me. I gaze behind to see the serpent lining up another strike.

Thor's hammer slams into the side of the serpent. Instead of grabbing Jormungandr's attention, it aggravates the serpent more. A pointy rock juts out of the ground, poking the serpent. Zildryss's distraction is also unable to deter the serpent's attack on me.

A flash of gold obstructs my view of the serpent. My heart stops when I realize it's Elan blocking the serpent's attack. Her posture is filled with determination to protect me.

"No, Elan!" I yell, suddenly finding more energy now that I need to protect my friend. I spin, maneuvering around her large body, and peg my sword, aiming directly for the serpent's eye. It lands true.

Jormungandr squeals and pulls back his head, my sword sticking out of his eye. I call to the sword with my magic, and it slowly backs out of the eye, causing more pain as it retracts. When the tip of the sword is free, the serpent squeals again, and I dare not take my attention from the serpent as I direct my sword back to my hand.

My fingers firmly wrapped around my sword's hilt, I glower at my dragon. "Don't you dare do that again! Don't you dare put yourself in harm's way to save me from something like that! Even with your size and ferocity, you don't stand a chance against the serpent."

Elan straightens her neck and stares down at me. *Ha. Try and stop me.* She spins, her tail thumping down next to me as she snarls up at the serpent. *Come on, serpent! You want a piece of this? Come and get it!* She charges the serpent, still writhing in pain.

The dragons continue their attacks, making the cut wider. The wound looks atrocious. That must be extremely painful, yet the serpent refuses to give up. I'm certain he won't give up until we damage his vital parts.

Elan runs up to the dragon and launches herself at his neck, ripping off more skin. The serpent's beady eyes narrow on her, and he recoils, his head jerked from side to side as each dragon grabs another chunk of flesh. Jormungandr flicks his tail and body, sending the other dragons flying. During all this commotion, the serpent's eye remains narrowed on my golden dragon.

Go, Elan! Take off to the sky. You can't let him get you, I yell through our bond so there is no mistaking that she will hear me. *You're playing with fire remaining there.*

Elan pushes off, her wings working profusely to get away from the serpent. She ascends quickly, but it's not quick enough to outfly the serpent's strike.

"No!" Devastation soaks my voice, and I want to collapse under the weight. Still, I can't tear my eyes away even though I don't want to see my beautiful companion killed. The dedication to be with Elan until the very last moment is strong.

Elan's in the direct line of fire, even with her golden wings working hard to escape. I push her with magic, yet it only seems to nudge her slightly. Mouth wide, exposing his fangs and ready to secure a dragon, Jormungandr closes in at a rapid pace, and I can do nothing to stop it. My sword squeals loudly as I rip it from its sheath and throw it at the serpent's other eye. Using my magic, I direct it point first. The sword flies true, following my instruction. I grit my teeth, hoping it will make it there in time.

Elan's wingbeats seem slow and lethargic,

completely opposite to the adrenaline-fueled effort I know she is making to get out of the way of the attack.

Like a lightning bolt, Eingana shoots down from the sky, aiming straight for my beautiful dragon. Her wings tucked by her side, head pointed down, she's nosediving straight toward her daughter. She flies close to the serpent's eyes, my sword narrowly missing her. I hold back my sigh of relief. She's not out of danger yet. The leader of the dragons flips so her feet hit Elan first and the collision slows her fall.

Elan is shoved off to the side from the force of the blow, and my beautiful dragon careens out of control to the outer circle. Eingana's fall slows almost to a halt, and Jormungandr clamps down on Eingana, his fangs piercing her scales. I hear several loud cracks that sound suspiciously like breaking bones, and my knees shake. Jormungandr tosses Elan's mother in his mouth then clamps down again with more sickening cracks. With a thud, Mjollnir passes under Jormungandr's neck and slams straight into the serpent's spine, disconnecting it from the rest of his body.

Jormungandr's head flies to the side, secured only by tendrils of flesh. With Eingana in his mouth, he falls slowly to the ground. Mouth falling open, he releases Eingana from his grasp. She tumbles to the side, rolling until the momentum stops her, and she lies motionless. Eingana's wings drape lifelessly over her, hiding some of her wounds.

"No," I breathe. "No," I say louder, and I bolt toward Elan's mother, the guilt digging its claws into me over discussing this possibility in a lighthearted manner earlier today. I feel as though I may have jinxed her. My legs don't work fast enough as I run toward her golden form. If there's any life left in her, I may be able to start some healing until Loki or Anita come to finish the job.

The nearby dragons land around their leader, blocking my view. Running, my feet stumble on rocks, and I work hard to regain my balance. More dragons, many injured, land to check on their leader, crowding me. We have defeated the serpent, yet the cost has been high. Very few of these magnificent creatures remain unscathed.

Hel's dark clouds loom over us ominously, enveloping us with the devastation and sadness of the scene before us. They release their energy in precipitation droplets, drenching all hopes that Eingana will be all right. Thick and heavy fog creeps in around the edges. The scene Hel is creating seems fitting for my current mood.

Zildryss lands on my shoulder then weaves around my neck to look me directly in the eyes. His eyes are wide and filled with grief, and I struggle to swallow my worry. Slowly, the little dragon curls around my neck then rests on my shoulder. His silence is concerning. He hasn't pressed against my neck to pass on his findings over the leader's fate, and this is making me nervous.

Is Mother all right? The pain in Elan's voice cuts through my heart like a knife. *She's not answering me.*

My heart weeps for her. She must be beside herself. My feelings pass through my mind speak. *Oh, Elan. I don't know. I'm sorry. I'm trying to get there.* I dodge past a few more dragons. *Are you okay?*

I'm injured, but nothing that won't heal. Just get to Mother.

Chapter Seventeen

Finally, I reach the last circle of dragons and weave my way through their legs to the inner edge of the ring surrounding Eingana. The distress passing through the dragons vibrates through the air. In the center, the beautiful leader of the dragons, an almost spitting image of Elan, lies unmoving, sprawled on the ground.

Meeting the eyes of the blue dragon opposite me, I ask, "Is she breathing?"

A shadow passes through the dragon's blue eyes as he gazes from me to Eingana, then at the little dragon sitting on my shoulders.

A red dragon on my right moves forward and places her nose an inch away from Eingana's nostrils. Worry burns deep in those red eyes. *I don't believe she is. I can't feel anything coming out.*

Holding my breath, I swallow. "Is there a heartbeat?"

The red dragon shakes her head, her red eyes turned down, eyeing her leader. *I'm afraid I can't hear her heart. It's usually a thunderous thump.*

Zildryss makes a depressed noise and presses the crown of his head against my neck. He doesn't portray any visions, but I'm suddenly overcome with grief.

Circling to the front, I embrace Eingana's large golden nose between my palms. It's still warm, her eyes are closed, and no life shines out of her skin. Every muscle in her body is lax and lifeless.

Tears blur my vision. "No." I choke on the word. "No," I repeat in a whisper. "No, no, no, no, no!" My voice crescendos, opening the well of tears. They stream freely down my face. I can't imagine having to tell Elan this. This is horrible. No wonder Zildryss didn't want to tell me. This is breaking my heart, and I'm going to destroy Elan's when I tell her the news.

Not Eingana. Not the leader of the dragons and my beautiful dragon's mother. The torment circles through my mind. I cling to the final shred of hope. "Wake up, Eingana. You can't leave us!" As an individual being, she is no more important than any other dragon. Still, the dragons have lost a respectable leader, and my best friend has lost her mother.

Eingana lies on one side, and I crawl between her front legs, pressing my back against her enormous chest, and relax my limbs next to her impressive size. Threading a hand under one of her leg scales, I close my eyes and attempt to control my emotions before I need to see Elan.

Well? Elan's voice echoes through my head.

A deep frown crinkles my forehead, and I ball myself into the fetal position, lying still. I don't want to respond, despite knowing I'll need to tell her eventually. I'm surprised another dragon hasn't told her.

Kara? The pain in Elan's voice makes me curl into a tighter ball. *Are you going to tell me what's happening?*

Just hearing her voice is breaking my heart. This is not right. I can't tell her. I just can't. Even if she has probably guessed. For the first time since we met, I ignore her. Deep down, I know it's probably best coming from me and most likely why the dragons haven't told her yet. Still, it's going to snap her heart in two when she finds out her mother died saving her. The grief would be bad enough just knowing that her mother had died.

I don't know how much time passes before the dragons start to file past their leader. They watch me still curled between Eingana's front legs as they touch their noses to hers—a symbol of respect as they say their farewells. When completing their goodbyes, the dragons move to the side.

Rocks scatter, and I hug my knees closer to my

chest, pressing my back against Eingana's scales, sealing my eyes shut. Wet streams carved by tears run down my face. More rocks scatter, and the dragons shift around me. I open my eyes a sliver to find the dragons have pulled aside, and down the path they've made, Elan scrapes her battered and bruised body along the ground. Seeing her like that breaks my heart all over again, and I crawl to my feet and head toward her.

Her eyes skim past me and land on her mother, worry filling every part of her face and eyes. *Kara, what's going on?*

I wouldn't be surprised if, deep down, she already knows but needs to hear it before she will believe it.

She studies her mother. *Why is no one healing Mother? She's not moving. She must be hurt. Why aren't you drawing the venom out of her system? You need to get to work before it's too late.*

Tears run down my face. Elan can't walk or fly, yet her mother is all she is thinking about. Elan is the one who needs healing, not her mother. The words form in my head to tell her, yet the enormous lump in my throat stops me from saying them. I shake my head and wipe my tears from my chin.

I revert to mind speak. *I'm sorry, Elan. She's*

gone. As soon as the words leave my head, tears run freely down my cheeks and drip over my chin while I watch the emotions play across Elan's face.

What do you mean she's gone? I can see her right there in front of me. Frustration creeps into her eyes and face.

She didn't make it. Jormungandr killed her. I place a hand on her nose.

Elan shakes her head. *No! No, she can't have died protecting me. It's not allowed.*

More tears stream down my face as I watch Elan trying to make her way closer to her mother. One wing droops sideways, broken in many places, and by the way that she is struggling to move, her legs are also hurt. She's not using her back legs at all, making me worried that they are broken.

She skims her stomach along the ground, trying to make it to her mother. *Can't someone heal her?*

Eyes wide and filled with sorrow and grief, I shake my head with small movements. *I'm sorry. I'm so sorry.*

Straining with all her effort, Elan slowly approaches Eingana and lowers her head to face her mother with their noses touching. She emits a faint wailing sound, letting it crescendo as time ticks by. Never have I heard this high-pitched sound come out of the dragons before. There is so much heartache filling that keen that it breaks my heart again.

Placing my hand underneath a scale on Elan's back, I started healing, pushing aside my exhaustion. She is battered, bruised, and needs healing in many places, yet all she can think about is her mother—her mother, who died to save her. As her keening continues, I inject healing power into her soft skin, sending it through her body.

It should have been me, not her. It should have been me, she says.

I rub my fingers in circles on the soft part of her skin. *She saved you so you could be the leader of the dragons. You are her next in line. You are the one that must take over when she passes, and she wanted you to live to do that. Mourn, then honor her wish.*

Elan throws back her head, facing the sky, and roars, loud and clear, filled with mourning. Each dragon around her lifts their face to the sky and imitates her, taking a moment to mourn their extraordinary leader.

When the grief has subsided, Elan lowers her head and touches her nose against her mother's and whispers again, *It should have been me.*

Pushing aside my own heartbreak, I look after my beautiful friend. She needs me now more than ever.

Leaving her to process her emotions, I set to work, targeting individual parts of her body to heal, knowing I have no magical power that can heal her heart.

Chapter Eighteen

E lan is too grief-stricken by her mother's death to let me get to the more significant parts of her body. So I start with her wings—healing the smaller bones that I can reach without asking her to move. Elan doesn't move. Her head rests on her front talons, and her nose remains pressed against her mother's.

Somehow, we have to notify her siblings as well. I haven't seen Sobek for quite some time. He and their other siblings are probably fighting farther down the field near the lava monsters.

Zildryss edges away from my neck and climbs down my arm and toward Elan's face. He rubs against the soft part of her nose then snuggles against her horns. His tail hooks under a smaller scale, and he seems to rest it against the soft skin underneath. Knowing the little dragon, he is probably doing his best to comfort her. The little dragon curls around her horn and closes his eyes, seemingly going to sleep.

Time ticks by, and the screaming, grunts, and moans mixed with the clashing of weapons keep me alert to the fighting in the background, robbing me of any comfort. I should be out there fighting and protecting Asgard. Even so, surely there are enough on our side that they don't need me for this moment while I help my best friend grieve and heal before getting back on her feet. The dragons need Elan to lead them.

Some rocks clatter around me, and I pull my eyes away from Elan to look up. The dragons remaining from the fight with Jormungandr edge closer to us. Leading the way is a brown dragon that looks much like Drogon, only there is more maturity around his features and in his eyes.

The brown dragon approaches slowly, his head down and horns pointing aggressively in our direction. He appears threatening until I look into his eyes. They are clouded with sympathy and grief.

Great Leader? His voice is gruff and deeper than Drogon's, showing signs of age.

Staring at him blankly, I blink.

He bobs his head, eyes fixed on Elan, and repeats himself. *Great Leader?*

Reality hits me, and I suck in a quick breath. He's

talking to Elan, not her mother. I nudge Elan, only to be ignored.

The brown dragon moves closer, and with respect lacing his voice, he says, *Great Leader?*

Elan doesn't respond. It's as though she's not even here. Her mind has gone off with her mother, trying to search for her in the land of the lost.

I touch Elan on her nose and stroke her just above her eye, trying to catch her attention. Her eyes are barely even open. The slits focus solely on her mother.

I try again. *Elan, they're calling you.*

She looks at me with droopy eyes filled with disbelief. *No, they're not. They're calling my mother.*

My heart caves with the words that must be said. Pumping all the warmth into my words, I say, *No, Elan. They're calling you. You are now the leader. Remember?*

Something flickers in Elan's eyes, and she blinks before slightly lifting her head to my eye level, gazing from me to the brown dragon.

The brown dragon sees he has her attention, and he repeats again, *Great Leader.* He lowers his head, touching his chin to the ground. *I am sorry for your loss. But we await your instructions.*

Elan blinks numerous times again. *What instructions?*

The brown dragon stands tall. *You are now our leader. You must tell us what you want us to do.*

When Elan stares at him blankly, he prompts her, *Do you want us to continue to fight and protect Asgard? Or do you want us to take your mother's body back to the dragon wastelands?*

Sadness distorts Elan's face. *Oh.* Slowly her gaze passes over the dragons, one at a time.

Eyes turned down, each dragon bows, touching their chin on the ground in respect, before standing tall, awaiting her instructions. In unison, they say, *We are sorry for your loss.*

I continue to work on Elan's wings, watching my friend closely as she processes everything around her.

Elan straightens, lifting her head as high as possible while still bound to the ground by her injuries. *I would like you to follow my mother's last instructions. We need to continue fighting for Asgard. Protecting Asgard is also protecting our homeland.*

Without wasting a moment, the dragons push into the sky and head down the battlefield to attack the other monsters, leaving the lifeless Midgard serpent across the ground. Something brown catches the corner of my eye, and I glance over to find Fenrir sitting on his haunches, curiously eyeing his dead brother before gazing at Thor, Elan, then me. He studies the battle farther down the open plain as if thinking things through. The hound then turns on his heel and leaves the area. He had promised Hel he wouldn't fight against her, and he also didn't want to fight against his father. The hound appears committed to his promise as he runs away without looking back.

Thor groans and slumps against a boulder, and Mjollnir drops to the ground beside him. As I continue to heal Elan, I keep an eye on him in my peripheral vision, ready to help him if he needs it. When he groans again, I rise to my feet to see if he needs aid.

The god holds up a hand at me. "No, stay there. Heal Elan. She needs it more. I'm just exhausted. That last hit took it out of me, and when my hammer returned, it hit my hand with such force, it knocked me against the boulder." He reaches up and flinches when he rubs the back of his head. "My head's got a good lump on it, but it'll be fine, eventually. You know how it is." One side of his mouth lifts, and he glances at Elan. "All brawn and no brains. Hey, eating companion?" His tone is bright, as if he's trying to cheer her up, though his body is obviously tired and weary.

Elan doesn't respond. After giving Thor a sad smile, I continue to work on her wounds. The god of thunder groans loudly as he pushes himself off the boulder and stumbles before leaning down to pick up his hammer. He staggers toward us. I gaze over at him as I continue healing Elan, glad to see he's okay. Despite the prophecy saying that he will be demolished by the Midgard serpent, it hasn't happened. Perhaps the prophecy won't come true at all. This gives me hope that Asgard won't fall.

Thor goes to Elan's side and threads his hand underneath her scale, touching her soft skin, just like I do. I'm shocked to see the tenderness he displays in that movement. My fondness for him grows deeper. My leader has treated me well, seeing past Odin's criticisms.

He runs his other hand down Elan's snout. "I'm sorry, eating buddy. This is not what I wanted to happen." The sympathy in his voice is overpowering, and I know he means every word. "I'm sorry you've lost your mother."

It was supposed to be me, not her, Elan repeats, her eyes constricted with grief.

Thor strokes the soft skin of her nose. "I know you think that, but I know for sure that your mother died to protect you because she was proud of you and thought you were ready to rule the dragons." He runs another hand up her snout. "And to be honest, I think you are too." His smile is sad as he looks into her heartbroken golden eyes. "You have grown greatly over the last few years. And for your young age, you are very mature. As much as I love your spark and enthusiasm, you will rule the dragons differently from your mother, but I'm sure it'll be in a way that you should be proud of."

He rubs a fist gently on the tip of her nose in a slight tussle. "I know you're hurting, but you need to push that aside for now. Just for the moment." He levels his gaze with her. "Now, let Kara heal you so you can get back into the battle and lead your dragons. They need to see you're strong."

Elan protests, *But I'm not strong. I'm broken.*

With a firm gaze, the god of thunder says, "No. Your heart is broken, not you. And you can still lead with a broken heart." Thor nudges her lightly with his hammer. "Come on. Let's lead these dragons. I will make sure Eingana is recognized throughout all Asgard." He stands. "You must remember that it's because Eingana executed your idea that we killed the Midgard serpent. We no longer have to deal with him and the mischief he causes."

Thor nudges her slightly harder. "Now, come on, eating buddy. Let's get going."

Elan rolls to her side, groaning with pain as she reveals her broken legs. *Can you heal me, please, Kara? These hurt so much.*

Chapter Nineteen

Thor runs, flinging his hammer loose as draugar head toward him. He still has a slight limp after I gave him a quick healing session, enough for him to move freely. The force of the hammer drives the draugar back, and when Thor catches it again, he summons lightning from the sky. The bright silver light flashes down, hitting several undead at once. From where I sit, healing Elan, this display is like our own private show tempered only by grief. Elan's face remains full of sorrow, but slowly, a steel reserve grows on her features as she readies herself to get back into battle.

My energy is completely depleted by the time I'm finished healing her. I don't know how I'm going to face another battle. Zildryss lands on my shoulders, startling me with his renewed energy after his nap on Elan. He pounces off my shoulder and sinks more draugar into the ground, working in unison with

Thor as the god of thunder wallops other undead and sends them flying.

I face Elan after healing her and offer a weak smile. "Are you all right to go, Elan?"

Elan stretches, extending her limbs to their full length. *I must get going, or my mother's death will be for naught. I'm not going to let that happen.* After one last nuzzle at her mother's nose, she climbs to her feet and looks down at me. *More like, are you ready to go?*

I slump on the spot and have trouble gathering enough energy to get to my feet. "I'm so exhausted after healing everybody in this enormous fight, especially after trekking everywhere."

Elan nudges me with her nose, and I grab onto her scales, using her strength to pull myself up. *I'm not surprised.* She lowers her stomach to the ground so I can reach the stirrups. *Jump on.*

It takes a lot of effort to climb onto her back, and after several attempts, I manage to hook my foot over the other side of the saddle and strap myself in. After I wrap my cloak around myself, Elan turns invisible. With exhaustion lacing my voice, I say, "Come on, dragon leader. Let's go show them how it's done."

Elan jumps and takes to the sky, only taking a few beats of the wings for her to get to a level high enough to observe all the dragons and everyone fighting. Thor slashes his hammer through the undead, with Zildryss sinking many more, while the angels of death slice off the heads of many more. It looks like they're getting somewhere now that they've got the extra dragons from the fight with Jormungandr on their side, plus Thor to help.

The Midgard serpent remains unmoving in the background, and ahead, Hel is framed by her lava monsters and hellhounds. The destruction they cause is significant, although, with the addition of more dragons to aid the Valkyries and elves, the odds are growing more in our favor. Each monster picked off is helping us.

A little flash of purple swoops past as Zildryss works his way toward the lava monsters. With renewed vigor, he attacks the monsters. He flies toward the lava monsters and circles behind them before landing and shooting his tail into the ground, sinking them up to their necks. It will be impossible for them to escape with their arms pinned to their side unless Hel calls them up.

Hel waves, directing her monsters to do her bidding as a dark cloud shrouds us, closing in on the battle and turning everything dark. I connect with Elan's dragon sight and oversee the dragons as they continue their fighting. Off to the side, I spot Loki in the form of Gilroma, still healing the dragons that have been struck by lava monsters. It's surprising to see him still working for our side. At the moment, his help is invaluable.

Zildryss drops another lava monster, and Thor fries a few more draugar with his lightning. Hel strains to raise one of her buried lava monsters from the ground. She manages to raise a few, yet the little dragon follows her progress and buries each monster again. He seems to be burying them with surprising ease, faster than Hel can raise them.

The Valkyries and gods continue their fight against the lava monsters, their swords piercing as far as they can into the stone-like monsters filled with boiling lava. Some blades dig a hole deep enough to reveal the lava within their stomachs, the metal often melting to liquid.

I search the ground for my friends and see a weary Naga back fighting, with Eir on his back. Drogon is ramming his horns into any lava monster he can, and Tanda flies to the sky and swoops down, picking up undead and ripping their heads off before dropping them to the ground.

A lava monster falls, and I'm surprised when I witness that he's completely split in half after the gods, einherjar, elves, and Valkyries have worked as one, driving their swords into them as the dragons pull them from the sides and rip them apart. Lava spills down their sides and to the ground. All the attackers fall to the sides, getting out of the way of the scalding lava.

The fleshy side of Hel's face is paler than I remember when she throws her hands up, trying to control her monsters and get them to stand and fight against us.

Movement catches my eye at the hole of the World Tree, and my cheeks turn numb. We are finally starting to gain control, but we don't need any more monsters to invade Asgard. Steeling my resolve, I glance at the trunk to see blue frost giants climbing out of the trunk. I grit my teeth, hoping they are here to help protect Asgard. Their loyalty could go either way. The first blue giant approaches the closest battle group and smashes a lava monster across its face. Inwardly, I cheer. They are on our side. Many more frost giants climb out of the hole, followed by humans from Midgard. Last of all, dwarves struggle over the lip of the hole. We have more backup, and the newcomers are quick to join in the battle. Freya's message must have reached everyone.

When Hel sees representatives from all the other realms pouring through the tree, the fleshy side of her face turns ghostly white, and her mouth falls open. It's still difficult to get used to her evenly balanced, half flesh, half skeletal features.

Following my instruction, Elan lands not far from

the goddess of Helheim, keeping us invisible. Climbing off Elan, I instantly turn visible and move to stand near Hel, pulling back my hood. "I think it's time you left, Hel."

Even though her side is fighting a losing battle, she looks down at me over her nose. "Who do you think you are to tell me what to do? You are merely a Valkyrie. You're not even a god."

"Yes, that is true. I'm only a Valkyrie, yet I can certainly see that you are on the losing side. More allies have come to help us."

As soon as the words leave my mouth, more from the other realms climb through Yggdrasil's hole. Many of the monsters around us are either getting buried, slaughtered, or bound by magic. The dwarves brought many of their magic-blessed weapons, and the items cut through the monsters with ease. They're even cutting through the lava monsters' stone exterior with little effort.

Indicating around me, I say, "As you can see, you're about to lose all your minions. Why don't you pull back and return to Helheim and send the lava monsters to Muspelheim?"

"I would do as she says, Hel." Thor stands behind me, his hammer in hand. "This is our realm, and you're trespassing. Not only that, but you're also losing. I suggest you take what is left of your minions and leave." He tosses his hammer, flipping it in one hand like a circus trick.

Hel's dark eyes dart from one section to the next, assessing the situation. Unrest spreads over her features before she backs away, inching toward the World Tree. Her eyes land on Thor. "You have not seen the last of me."

Thor crosses his arms, his biceps bulging under his jerkin. "You no longer have the support of your brother, Jormungandr, and Fenrir just wants to live in peace with his father, you, and Tyr. Go back to Helheim and stay there. Don't come back. If you don't disturb us, we won't disturb you."

Hel lifts her chin. "And what about your brother, Balder? Aren't you going to continue hassling me for him?"

Thor's sigh is full of disappointment. "As much as I would like my brother back—and my mother would certainly like him back—I know that you will not release him. So it's best if we leave him for now. If you treat him well, we will not come to get you or him." He runs his fingers through his matted red hair. "Although I know it will break my mother's heart."

Hel backs off to Yggdrasil and climbs over the edge of the hole. The dark, ominous clouds and their misty moisture follow her. They disappear behind her, leaving Asgard in its normal dry form. The remaining monsters eventually realize their leader has gone, and they follow her out of our realm. The warriors ensure that every lava monster, draugar, and hellhound leaves the realm. When peace finally returns, we are left to assess the carnage.

- Chapter Twenty -

With the help of the other realms, we start cleaning up and search for friends. Many creatures of all sizes and realms are lost in sorrow after finding friends and loved ones injured or deceased on the sides. Keening fills the atmosphere with despair, tainting our victory with mourning. So many have lost their friends and relatives. Faint hope shines in the eyes of the searchers, desiring to see their friends' faces healthy and alive.

In the distance, Thor, still limping, is checking through the gods. I didn't notice all the fresh battle wounds covering him when he stood behind me to tell Hel to leave. His face is swollen and covered in bruises mixed with blood; dark venom mats his hair and bushy beard. Mjollnir tucked in the back of his belt, he passes over all the fallen, helping the injured gods and friends struggling to move.

None of my healing energy remains, and I haven't

had the necessary time to recharge, making me feel helpless. I almost cheer with delight when I spot Anita, the healer from the Valkyrie Academy, as she continues to work on as many beings as she can.

I search for my friends. Since I saw them alive and well earlier, a lot has happened, and my stomach churns with worry. I scan each and every face of the Valkyries and dragons. Between the five types of dragons, it's hard to easily pick out my dragon friends by their colors, as each color has its own distinct shape. Telling the difference is similar to distinguishing between identical twins. Only the small features make them recognisable.

"There you are."

A familiar voice behind me fills my heart with joy. I spin and smile broadly when I find Eir with Naga not far behind.

"Oh. Thank Vanir! I've been so worried for all of you. Have you seen the others?" I wrap her up in a hug, and she winces. I pull back, observing her. "Are you okay?"

She brushes me off affectionately. "Yes, I'm all fine. It's just minor bruises and scratches. It'll heal fine." She nods to the left. "There's Tanda and Britta."

Spinning, I spot our friends sifting through the injured. Britta spends time squatting and healing several of the wounded with Tanda never leaving her side as though still in protective mode. After catching Britta's eye, I sigh with relief and approach her. "Oh. I'm so happy to see you. What about Hilda? Have you seen her?"

Yes, she's seen us, a gruff voice says. I turn to find Drogon's nose in line with my stomach. He nudges my stomach, missing me with his horns.

I smile. "Drogon, it's so good to see you."

His horns are covered with muck and goo, looking rather unpleasant. I look past the mess to find Hildr sitting on his back. Her spiky red hair is in disarray, giving her exhausted face a strange look.

The Valkyrie swings her leg over the side and drops to the ground with a thud. "It's good to see you too. I'm relieved that everyone made it to the other side."

I shake my head. "You have no idea how happy I am to see all of you."

A worried look distorts Eir's normally peaceful face as she searches our shoulders then the sky. "Have you seen Zildryss?"

I chuckle, and her worry turns to confusion. "Zildryss is an amazing little dragon that has been able to defend himself... mostly. He buried so many of our enemies, it's ridiculous. That little tail of his did wonders."

As if hearing his name, Zildryss squeaks and

lands. He runs around Eir's shoulders before rubbing up against her neck.

Her chuckle is ecstatic while she runs a finger over his lilac scales. "It's good to see you too, little guy."

Each of my friends has bruises and cuts all over them. Their faces and hair are covered in gunk, yet none of this can take away how happy I am to see them.

"Now that I know everyone's okay, I'm going start healing more of the injured," Eir says. "Do any of you need healing?"

I shake my head. "I'm physically exhausted to the bone. Otherwise, I'm fine. Unless you have a cure for a broken heart?"

A cloud of worry crosses Eir's face. "What do you mean?"

Britta approaches and joins the group.

Watching Elan's reaction, I explain, "Eingana didn't make it."

Elan's head drops, and grief soaks her face as soon as the words leave my mouth.

Britta stops healing and looks at Elan. "Really?"

"What happened?" Hildr asks.

Saddened by Elan's grief, I stroke her nose, trying to comfort her. "She dived in front of the Midgard serpent to protect Elan." I look to the ground, my hands shaking with grief. "The serpent got her instead." Sidling up to Elan, I press the side of my face against her hard scales. "If she hadn't done so, Elan wouldn't be with us. But because she did, that leaves Elan as leader of the dragons."

Drogon, Tanda, and Naga bow until their chins touch the ground.

Tanda's red eyes are earnest as she looks Elan in the eye. *We're so sorry for your loss, Elan. Your mother was an outstanding leader, and I'm sure you will be too.*

Elan doesn't answer and remains fixed on the spot, drenched in grief.

Naga knows that Elan will be a very good leader. Naga is very sad Eingana is gone, but Naga is happy his friend will be the leader. The blue dragon nudges Elan, and she affectionately presses the side of her head against him.

Thank you, Naga, Elan says. *I'm happy that I have you three with me as well as our Valkyrie friends. And, of course, Zildryss.* She casts the little dragon a warm look.

I rub her cheek. "You're not alone, Elan. We will be here with you."

"We're also sorry for your loss," Eir says. "I wish I could heal your heart. Although if I could, I don't think you would be able to remember your mother the way you should. It's hard, yet best if we process our grief and learn to live with it daily." She cups Elan's nose between her palms. "I'll be here as a friend anytime you need me. First, I must go and try to heal everybody who is still alive and injured."

Elan nods. *Of course.*

Britta and Hildr excuse themselves and set to work helping Eir heal the injured.

I'll check on all the dragons, Drogon says. *I'll check on the damage to our kind and see who may need help.*

I'll go also, Tanda says.

And Naga will go too, the blue dragon adds. *We will check on everyone and see what we can do.*

I reach for the blue pendant around my neck, drain it of any remaining magic, and touch the soft part of Elan's skin, pumping a small amount of healing magic into her, hoping I can help her feel better.

"I going to have a look around too," I say.

If you're going around, then so am I, Elan says.

Weaving through all the injured, I'm devastated by the sight of the destruction. At least we have healers equipped to help them. Hopefully, their energy will hold until all the significant healing is done. Eventually, I stumble across Loki, still in the form of Gilroma, healing another dragon.

My feet halt. "You're still here?"

He focuses his glowing yellow eyes on me, and a

shiver runs down my spine. There are so many emotions attached to those eyes. "You're saying that a lot, Kara."

Reminding myself that it's only Loki, I shrug. "What can I say? Usually, you've taken off by now and gone somewhere else and left us alone in a mess."

Loki ponders for a moment before tilting his head to the side. He runs a hand over his tattooed scalp. "I guess I deserve that. Although, as you know, I have a lot of making up to do. So, here I am. Perhaps Odin will give me the award for being the most loyal." He smiles, and the cheekiness looks creepy in Gilroma's form.

"Yeah. Good luck with that," I say. "I'm happy to see that you've stuck around for a change. We need your help."

Chapter Twenty-One

The majority of the injured are transported to the infirmary for long-term care until they are well enough. Others with non-life-threatening injuries receive first aid then help sort out the mess of the deceased and the trashed land. Bodies are gathered and lined up in long lines.

"May I have everyone's attention?" Odin claps loudly, perched on top of a large boulder, his burgundy cape torn in many places and his face speckled with cuts and grime. His two ravens land on each shoulder and whisper in his ear.

The creatures and beings from every realm gather around the foot of the boulder. Frost giants stand tall, towering over everyone and making the dwarves seem smaller. The usual look of hatred or distrust is put aside after the combined effort to rescue the worlds.

Slowly, Odin spins in a full circle, his one eye

taking in all the people and creatures around him. His face bears a rare look of gratitude and serenity as he adjusts his black eyepatch. "I would like to thank everyone here for your help. I know that our realms have not always seen eye to eye." Odin's gaze lands on the frost giants and the dark elves before continuing on to the Vanir and other realms that are currently at peace with Asgard despite many previous disputes.

"In spite of our past troubles, you have all come together to save Asgard and, in return, possibly saved all of the realms attached to Yggdrasil," Odin says. "Your bravery and help are much appreciated, and because of this, I would like to declare you all friends of Asgard. It is my hope that we can live in peace in the future and that this battle has taught us something about living and working together."

He continues to address the different realms and their beings as he turns slowly in a circular motion. Odin holds up his hands in retreat as he recognizes some hardened faces in the crowd. "I know I have not always been the most patient of leaders. Please, bear with me as I try to work on this." A couple of the hardened faces soften, and he continues, "There have been many that I have held with strict disapproval, and I've treated them with disregard when their actions don't call for such a severe punishment." His eyes land on me. "Many of these people will be given credit for what they are due, and we will allow them the freedom to roam through Asgard and embrace them as friends."

The leader of the gods pauses, and his mouth turns into a thin line. "And there are others that shall be given more freedom." He holds up a finger. "But we will be watching closely as we do not completely trust what they do." His eyes land on Loki, who has returned to his god form, and the god of mischief has the decency to look slightly embarrassed. "These particular ones have helped a lot today, and this freedom shall be their reward."

He gazes past the crowd in front of him to all the deceased respectfully gathered by the living and lined next to each other in rows. "If you will allow, I will be happy to bury those who fought for us in this area as a reminder of what has taken place here. We will need some help from magical beings to bury them under this rocky surface. We would also ask for help from the dwarves to mark the gravesites with an honorable gravestone. We will treat each and every grave with the respect we would give our own."

His eyes fix on something in the distance, and he frowns. "We also need to address the remaining lava monsters. Many are still alive with their bodies buried and their heads remain above the surface. We need to finish them properly, bury them, and trap them with magical powers. We need to make sure they don't have powers of resurrection, emerge from the ground, and bring more havoc. Is there anybody here that can do that?"

A dwarf in the front calls, "Almost all the dwarves can do that." Many dwarves in the crowd nod and hum their agreement.

Odin clasps his hands together. "Fantastic! Then if you have enough energy, let's get to work. The bodies of the beings that defended us need to be set to rest. Are there more beings here that can help?" He looks around the crowd again.

"A couple of the Valkyries with magic can help." I run a finger over the lilac dragon's head, and he snuggles into me. "And little Zildryss here was the expert who buried them all when we fought."

Odin eyes us skeptically then nods once. "Very well. Please set to work as fast as you can."

The crowd begins to disperse, and Odin holds up his hands. "Wait!"

When everyone stops, he adds, "I forgot to mention. Because we all worked together to save the realms, I will be hosting a party tomorrow night on the grounds outside the palace. You are all welcome to come and celebrate this victory with us, and together, we will remember the loved ones lost." He smiles. "Thank you again for your help. Please, feel free to finish what you were doing, and we hope to see you tomorrow night."

Everyone sets to work gathering the deceased who hadn't been lined up ready for burial while others set to work burying them.

Zildryss and Eir walk beside me as we assess the situation and converse with the dwarves over the best plan of action for the deceased. My energy is still withered, but I should be able to drum up enough to start burying the bodies.

"If you lot bury them, we will set the head-stones," says a dwarf, peering over his glasses. There is something familiar about him, and it takes me a moment to realize he's one of the sons of Ivaldi from our trip to Svartalfheim, the creators of Fenrir's lead. I peer at the dwarf on his left and notice the balding brother running a hand through his few remaining strands of graying hair over the bald patch.

Zildryss flies off Eir's shoulders and lands on the ground, flipping his tail over his head and poking it into the ground. The first body in line is a dragon, and he sinks deep into the rocky ground. The dwarves conjure stone from the ground and set to work with the tools they had brought with them to the fight. They chisel the names and one-line descriptions given to them by the friend or loved one mourning over the being. The dwarves finish by embossing their magic into the stone and setting it into place in the ground above the head. The dwarves' work is impressive. Each headstone has its own individuality and emblems then embossed with magic to secure their work for centuries to come.

This ritual continues down the line. Eir, Zildryss, and I take turns burying, and the dwarves alternate creators for the headstones. Several dwarves take responsibility for interviewing the loved ones for the gravestones and arranging a small memorial. Each burial brings sadness to my heart. We have lost so many. I thank each one before they are sent deep into the ground. Their sacrifices have saved Asgard and many of the realms attached to Yggdrasil.

We work for hours, taking breaks to recoup our magic. I push through much exhaustion, and when we are completely drained of energy, we rest for the night. The frost giants stand guard over the bodies until we set to work again the following morning.

The next day after we start back at work, a harsh voice behind me asks, "Can I help with that?"

Turning, I spot the dark elf who trained us in Alfheim and introduced us to Zildryss. She has several bandaged areas on her limbs, but is otherwise in good shape. "I would've helped yesterday, but I was stuck in the infirmary. Healing isn't one of my specialties." She shrugs.

"Elaith!" Relief floods through me. "If you're up to it, that would be fantastic."

Eir braces her upper arm affectionately. "It's nice to see you again."

The dark elf grunts, always lax on showing kind emotion. She's about to set to work when she spots Zildryss landing on Eir's shoulder. The harshness in her face immediately disappears, her eyes softening at the tiny dragon. She strokes his cheek. "It's good to see you again, little guy."

Zildryss launches off Eir's shoulder and lands on Elaith's, curling against her neck and drooping his tail over her shoulder.

"Have they been good to you?" she asks him.

Zildryss presses his tummy against her skin, and a smile spreads across her face. It's a strange sight on the dark elf. "That's good. I'm glad they've been looking after you."

"Of course we've been looking after him." Eir sounds insulted. "This little guy has been a godsend. He has helped us in so many ways."

"Can I help you?" a cheerful voice asks. I have to blink twice and remind myself that this isn't Loki when I find Aymar, the podgy elf teacher from Alfheim. He was supposed to be our peaceful magic

150

teacher until Loki kidnapped him and took his form and place.

Although, I have to check. "Are you Loki or the actual peaceful magic teacher?"

The elf stiffens. "I'm the real elf. I know we didn't actually meet properly or spend time together, but this is me, not that treacherous god. He's over there, healing a couple of additional wounded."

I follow his pointed finger to see Loki still in his god form, working on healing the injured. I grin. "Sorry. I had to check."

The magic teacher's face softens. "I understand."

"You are certainly welcome to help us if you can do this. It's not the magic Loki taught us while in your form," I say.

The rounded elf holds his tummy and chuckles. "Easy." He squats beside a human next in line to be buried and sinks them deep into the rocky ground. Then the dwarves get to work setting the headstone.

Chapter Twenty-Two

Burying the many bodies takes most of the next day. To conserve our energy, we train Hildr and Britta on how to execute the burial as well. The Valkyries took a few goes to perfect the move until, eventually, they worked it out and could execute it without our help. If not for their help, we would have been working into the night.

While we were tending to the burials, the uninjured and healed dragons, with the help of the frost giants for the larger creatures, moved the injured beings to the infirmary in order of their injury's severity. The six realms worked together cleaning up the destruction. Although Jormungandr was left out to be eaten by the scavengers.

When we address Eingana, I make sure I'm by Elan's side. My heart hurts every time I see the lifeless form of Elan's mother and the leader of the dragons. It must be killing Elan to see her mother like that. Her face torn with grief, Elan sits by her side, and it looks like she hasn't moved since the war finished. When she spots us coming, my beautiful golden friend curls tighter next to her mother.

I move next to her, nestle against her large head, rest against her snout, and rub my hand along her scales. Eventually, I slide a hand under her scale to touch her soft flesh and inject her with peaceful magic. It's not much, but maybe it'll help. "Do Sobek and the rest of your family know?"

A low rumble of grief vibrates through her throat. *Yes, they know. They have gone back to the dragon wastelands to grieve and look after things there. Many dragons have returned to look after their young. I just can't face them yet.*

Exhausted, I lean closer to her, trying to regain my energy and thinking of the best way to honor Eingana.

Rolling over, I face her and feel her hot breath wash over me. "I know this won't be easy, but we need to bury her." I run my hand over Elan's nostrils. "Would you like her to be buried here? Or back in the wastelands?"

The grief I feel through our bond almost floors me. It is so overwhelming and heavy, an almost impossible burden to bear.

A tear leaks from the corner of my eye. "Oh, Elan,

I feel for you. I really do. I wish it went another way so that you both could live."

I know. Elan closes her eyes, hiding the hurt swimming in them. *She deserves a suitable burial. One that will honor her.*

"And we will make sure she gets it."

She opens her eyes a crack. *Thank you.*

"I'd have it no other way." I stroke the top of her nose. "Do you want her buried here or in the dragon wastelands?"

Again, the grief overwhelms me, and just thinking about it brings me to tears. I give her time to consider it. The others are still burying the last few deceased, giving me time to relate to Elan. Zildryss circles our heads before landing on Elan's neck and hangs between her horns. It's his favorite spot to act as though he is the king of the dragons. Elaith arrives with him, staying in the outskirts and giving us space. She's flanked by Drogon, Tanda, and Naga with their riders, Hildr, Britta, and Eir.

Zildryss rubs his belly along Elan's horns, and she shifts her head upright. Her eyes open wide, unfocused, then the little dragon lifts off again. Elan's eyes focus and tilt up as she tries to look at the tiny dragon between her horns. *That seems like a wonderful idea, Zildryss, if you can do that.*

"What does he want to do?" I ask.

Her eyes light up. *With Elaith's help, he wants to bury her and then build a big rock on top and name it Eingana's Rock.* Her voice brims with emotion.

I look up at the little dragon. "That's a fantastic idea, Zildryss. Can you do it?"

The tiny lilac dragon nods.

"Together, we will easily be able to do that," Elaith agrees with him.

"That's fantastic!" I stand and tug on Elan's leg. "Come on. We must move for them to be able to do that."

It takes a lot of effort for Elan to get up. Her movements are slow and riddled with grief. After she is on all fours, she touches her nose to Eingana's and briefly holds it there before backing away. *I'll miss you, Mother.*

Straightening, Elan projects her voice as though addressing a large crowd. *All the dragons that can make it here, come gather. We're going to bury my mother, and it'd be nice if you were here to show your respects to your leader.*

Within moments, the sky fills with different colors as dragons flock in from all directions. Even the dragons with broken wings scurry across the land from the infirmary. They gather around their new leader, each bowing in respect. Drogon, Naga, and Tanda flank Elan. Zildryss sits on her head between her horns as I stand underneath her. Hildr, Britta, and Eir stand by their dragons.

Elan stands tall. *We have decided to bury my beloved mother and the leader of the dragons of the wasteland here. A memorial of stone will be set over her grave and named appropriately.*

Zildryss flies off Elan's head and lands on the ground in front of Eingana, and Elaith joins him. They work together, with Zildryss burying his tail into the ground and sinking Eingana deep into the rocky surface. The dark elf conjures up a large boulder from the ground, much larger than Eingana's form. The strain on her body is evident as she molds many large rocks together, making sure they are secure and strong enough for a lifetime before she pulls the conjured boulder over the spot where Zildryss buried Eingana. The air is eerily silent, laced with grief, as they lay the beloved leader of the dragons to rest.

"Coming through. Coming through. Stand aside," gruff voices call, the owners hidden between the dragons' legs. "Excuse me. Yes, that's it. Move aside." The sons of Ivaldi barge through the dragons, their tools clenched in their fists. Their short bodies waddle up to the enormous boulder and use their tools to chip the surface. Slowly, words form, embedded into the side of the boulder in large decorative script. "Eingana's Rock. Leader and mother. Respected for her compassion, wisdom, and strength."

After the dwarves pack away their tools, the dragons face the boulder, throw their heads to the sky, and roar. The mournful wailing roar sends shivers right down to my feet.

My stomach swirling in knots, I cast a side-glance at Eir and whisper, "Well, that was intense."

Eir's eyes are wide as she nods.

When the wailing stops and the dragons have fallen silent, Naga climbs to the top of Eingana's Rock and peers down at his comrades before focusing on Elan. *Elan, you must come up here.*

She does as instructed, her face displeased about the attention, especially now. Still, she sucks up her responsibility and stands next to Naga. He wraps a wing over her back in what looks like a hug.

This rock honors our past leader, and Naga stands here in all respect as Naga wants to announce the new leader. The dragon's ribs expand as he takes a deep breath. *Naga is very proud to announce his friend Elan as our new leader. Naga asks all of you to salute Elan, our future leader, and support her in all her decisions, as you all did with an Eingana.*

Every dragon around us starts thumping their tail

against the ground, causing it to vibrate harshly, making it feel like there's an earthquake.

Elan pulls back her shoulders and raises her face to the sky, loosing an authoritative roar etched with grief.

Chapter Twenty-Three

A deep sadness swirls in Elan's golden eyes as she jumps off her mother's memorial rock with a thud, shaking the ground. She nudges me with her nose. *I'm sorry, my friend. I'm going to have to go away for a little while and help the dragons settle with me as the leader.*

I touch her nose and look deep into her big eyes. "I know. That doesn't mean I won't miss you like nothing else. Although I understand that you must go away for a while and establish your place within your dragon community."

She drops to all fours and puts her belly on the ground. I undo the straps of her saddle around her stomach, and she lifts her belly slightly, aiding me as I pull it off her from the side. Her eyes are fixed on me the whole time as though she is etching me into her memory. I give her a sad smile.

She tilts her head to the side. *Don't you ever forget*

if you ever need me, I will be here as soon as I can. This will only be for a little while. You're still my best friend. I'm bonded with you, and it's going to stay that way.

Tears trickle down my face as I run my hands over her snout. I force my voice past the lump in my throat. "I know. I'm going to miss you so much. I look forward to the day that everything is sorted, and we can be together again." I wipe my tears on my uniform. "Who knows? Maybe I should come to stay with you in the dragon wastelands for a while. We shouldn't have any more battles to fight for a while. Maybe Thor will give me leave time so I can help you settle in."

I would love that, but it's not exactly a friendly environment for a Valkyrie.

I smirk. "It's much friendlier than last time I stayed. The dragon-and-Valkyrie relationship has shifted for the better."

Elan grins, showing off her massive array of teeth that always look more ferocious than friendly, and it melts my heart. *You have that right. No one should try to eat you this time. Especially because you are my friend.* Her voice warms. *I would love for you to come and visit. If Thor will let you stay for a while, then please come. With you by my side, it will comfort me and make it easier for my heart to heal.*

I grin. "I'll be there as soon as I can." I tilt my

head to one side. "Although I hope we're not there forever because I like my friends too." I gaze over my shoulder at the other Valkyries.

Elan nudges me again, knocking me backward, and I struggle to stay on my feet. *Then I'll see you soon. Don't take too long. I miss you already.* She expels an enormous roar then projects into the air, flying toward the dragon wasteland with all the dragons taking off after her.

Naga's going to go with her too, and so are Drogon and Tanda. We want to make sure that Elan settles in well as our new leader, and we want to be there to support her. Naga leans into Eir as she throws her arms around his neck, tears brimming in her eyes. While Tanda and Drogon say goodbye to Britta and Hildr, both the dragons and Valkyries are overcome with sadness.

"Perhaps we should all go to the dragon waste-lands for a while," Britta says.

I would like that very much. Tanda's red eyes light with enthusiasm. *Except Elan says it's not the best place for people that aren't dragons. There's a minimal food supply, and you might get sick of eating meat all the time.*

Britta chuckles. "You've got that right."

"But Eir and I can teach you how to conjure up food with magic. Then the choice of food won't be a problem." I nudge Eir with my elbow.

Eir nods. "We learned that while we were on Alfheim."

Then that's even better, Tanda says.

The three large dragons take off back to their homeland.

Approaching slowly from the background, a tall elf with pale, freckled skin and auburn hair flowing past his shoulders moves toward Eir. His square jawline is set, and his green eyes are filled with empathy as he studies the peaceful Valkyrie. The elf shifts next to Eir and gently takes her hand.

Eir catches sight of the newcomer, and her face turns bashful.

"Who's this?" Britta's eyebrow rises.

Eir glances at the elf holding her hand, then back at Britta, her eyes wide. "This is my friend Taredd, from Alfheim."

Britta grins. "Friend, huh?"

I smile, observing Eir's discomfort. "Yes. He was Eir's love interest when we were on Alfheim."

Taredd smiles broadly and peers down at Eir. "I like the sound of that, as long as the love interest has continued."

Her cheeks bright red, Eir nods, and Taredd's smile somehow spreads wider. He squeezes her hand. "Are you coming to the party?"

A tinge of pink flashes through her cheeks. "Of course."

"Wonderful! I'll see you there," he says and grabs her other hand briefly before turning to leave.

THE FOUR VALKYRIES flock into the party together. Long flowing dresses drape to their ankles, clinging to their lithe, muscular forms from a shoulder strap. After wearing fighting leathers for so long, it's strange to walk in our open sandals, but at least we don't have to tackle high heels. I swipe a strand of my flowing black hair behind my ear to look at the other three. We all look so different. We're clean after such a long journey, all the dirt scrubbed from our faces.

Taredd spots us from the edge of the gathering, and his eye fix on Eir, never straying for a moment while working through the crowd toward her. He slips his hand in Eir's and whispers in her ear. His green peaceful eyes study every part of Eir's face as her face flushes, the color showing under the dim firelight illuminating the outer party area. Seemingly satisfied with her reaction, he pulls back and says, "Perhaps you can come to Alfheim for a while now that your responsibilities are finished."

Eir tilts her face up and runs a hand down his cheek. "I would like that. But first, I would like to see that Naga and the dragons are okay. And if Naga isn't needed on the dragon wasteland, I'd like to bring him with me. If that's okay?"

"Of course it is." He plays with the tip of her hair. "Just don't take too long. We haven't had enough time together."

"I promise." She looks at him openly, her expression seemingly fulfilled.

The elf wraps his arms around her from behind and rests his chin on top of her head, watching the action at the party. Loud groups of gods, warriors, and Valkyries mix with all the different beings from the five other realms, and much laughter fills the air. It's lovely to find all these realms congregating together and celebrating in unison. The only realms not represented are those ruled by Hel.

Although his cuts are cleaned and bruises reduced, they remain evident on Thor's face, illuminated by the firelight as he fills his mead cup to the top from the cauldron lying directly under Heidrun. The goat climbs the branches of Yggdrasil and chews its leaves, enabling her to produce mead rather than milk. The god of thunder weaves drunkenly through the crowd. I'm surprised he hasn't been yelling for me to fill his cup for him. On the other hand, my leader has never been a slavedriver and probably knows that I'm just as exhausted as he is. My heart warms at the memory of what we have been through lately. Never has he been disrespectful or doubted me.

As though sensing he is being watched, his eyes dart through the crowd and meet with mine. He raises his pewter cup in a salute before he looks behind me as though looking for Elan, his trusty eating companion. Sadness washes over his face before his eyes connect with mine again, and his shoulders droop momentarily. He makes his way to the eating table, where several giants and beings from other realms are holding an eating competition, and waits his turn. When I size up the frost giant sitting at the table, I figure he has someone to replace Elan for the moment.

Much laughter and merriment passes through the groups. On a makeshift dance floor, giants dance happily with dwarves and elves with humans. Freya dances sensually in the center of a group of gods with her angels of death lining the outskirts, ensuring their goddess remains safe, despite the friendly atmosphere. Even though they guard their goddess, many still take turns in joining in the festivity.

A voice projects loudly over the crowd as though

magically enhanced. Frigg stands on a small stage along the wall of Valhalla Hall. Her flowing blue gown hugs her curves and drapes to her ankles. Her demeanor is pleasant, yet an underlying sadness follows her like a ghost.

Odin's wife clears her throat again, capturing the attention of even the rowdy partiers. When satisfied she has everyone's attention, she begins, "As many of you know, my dearest son, Balder, died unexpectedly from one item that did not swear its loyalty to him and promise not to harm him."

The people sigh loudly with disappointment and regret, and Frigg holds up a hand. "I've come to the realization that it's my fault. Because it wasn't old enough and only a mere little vine, I thought it was nothing worth worrying about." She looks around the room. "As you know, Balder came to an untimely demise and didn't die as a warrior. Because of this, he's been sent to Helheim. As much as you all have taken part, I appreciate your efforts to release a tear of sorrow for him. Although we didn't get everyone's tear. There were ones that refused to cry."

A gasp of shock echoed through the room. "Even though we were very close to filling her request, Hel won't release his soul back to the land of the living."

Lots of murmurs of rage and disbelief echo through the crowd, egged on by too much mead.

"As much as it pains me, I've realized that he won't be coming back to us no matter what we do. As you've all seen, Hel is already mad with us and won't do us any favors." Frigg holds something in a lowered hand and raises it so everyone can see. She walks through the crowd, giving everyone a look at the thing in her hand.

"This little thing here is mistletoe. It's the one thing that did not swear a promise that it wouldn't harm him and happened to be Balder's demise." She paces some more, stopping by individual people and holding the little leaves close for them to see. "I would like to make something good of this. So, in honor of Balder, I would like to make this a sign for the god of light in showing our love for him. Balder was much loved by everyone. Because of this, I'd like to enforce a new rule." She stops in front of Eir, with Taredd's arms still wrapped around her from behind. Frigg holds the mistletoe high above them, displaying the expanse of dark green leaves and berries. "If this is hanging over the top of two people, then the couple must kiss." A sly look crosses her face as she eyes Eir and her elf.

Eir blinks, her light-brown eyes unsure. Taredd wastes no time. He twists her to face him, cups her chin in his forefinger and thumb, and gently draws her up for a kiss. Eir's cheeks turn bright red, and her eyes dreamy.

Hoots and cheers rattle through the crowd, especially from the warriors. Frigg remains in front of them, the mistletoe still held high, and a smirk of pleasure crosses her face. "Perfect. Just how I'd like my precious son to be remembered."

Get updates & notifications of giveaways

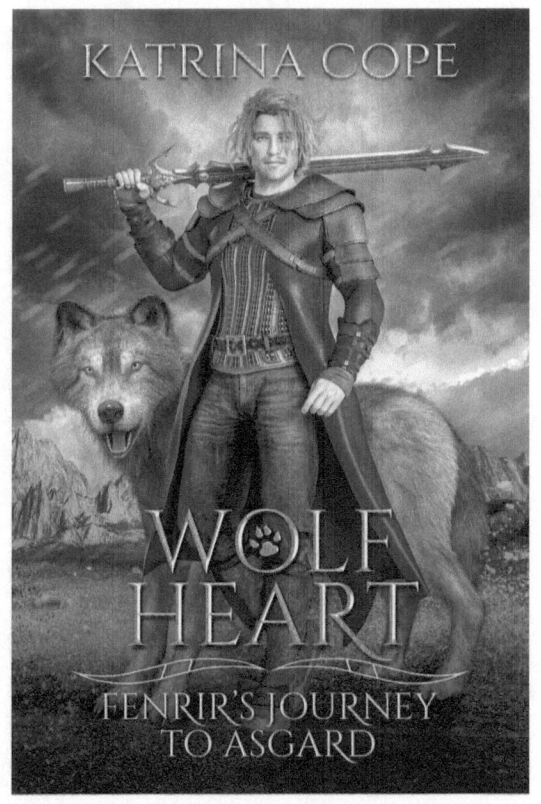

Would you like a FREE ebook?

Click here to get started: FREE copy of Wolf Heart: Fenrir's Journey to Asgard or go to https://BookHip.com/KQGGZF

Through this link you can sign up for my newsletter and

receive a FREE copy of Wolf Heart plus updates about my fantasy books, sales and notification of giveaways.

ACKNOWLEDGMENTS

It's sad to say goodbye to Kara, Elan and their friends. I have lived in their shoes for the last few years and it has been one action-packed ride.

Thank you to all of the creators of literature and websites who have spent time writing about Norse Mythology. Even though at times, there has been contradicting information, it has been an interesting study. After all, a goat produces mead, and a dragon gnaws at the roots of the Yggdrasil, unhindered, threatening the existence of the nine realms attached to the world tree. Plus, there are many other "believable" tales told.

Norse mythology is such an impressive set of tales that I have incorporated some and invented others to create Kara and Elan's story. It has been a fun journey living in the shoes of Kara, and her trusty dragon, Elan.

I'm touched by the enormous support I have received from my immediate family. My husband has been a helpful first reader and, at times, been an excellent motivator, with hints of ideas to help me through the blanks. The support from my three sons has also been overwhelming. They have spent years putting up with my head in the clouds, thinking about the next plot twist or story, along with many hours spent working on my books and keeping in touch with my readers.

A big thank you to my readers, who have loved the dragon and her rider and found the stories entertaining and funny.

A huge thank you to my editor, Stefanie B., for her editing and writing tips, and my proofreader, Irene S., for picking up the things we missed.

Thank you to all of my readers who have loved my work, and continue to read my stories.

BOOKS BY KATRINA COPE

Pre-Teen Books

The Sanctum Series

JAYDEN'S CYBERMOUNTAIN

SCARLET'S ESCAPE

TAYLOR'S PLIGHT

ERIC & THE BLACK AXES

ADRIANNA'S SURGE

~~~~~

Young Adult Urban Fantasy

Afterlife Series

FLEDGLING

THE TAKING

ANGELIC RETRIBUTION

DIVIDED PATHS

TRUTH HUNTER

Afterlife Novelette

THE GATEKEEPER

~~~~~

Young Adult Urban Paranormal Fantasy

Supernatural Evolvement Series

(Associated with the Afterlife Series)

WITCH'S LEGACY (Prequel)

AALIYAH

~~~~~

Young Adult Norse Mythology Fantasy

Valkyrie Academy Dragon Alliance

MARKED (Prequel)

CHOSEN

VANISHED

SCORNED

INFLICTED

EMPOWERED

AMBUSHED

WARNED

ABDUCTED

BESIEGED

DECEIVED

Thor's Dragon Rider

SAFEGUARD

PURSUIT

ENTRAPMENT

HOODWINKED

RELINQUISHED

SHROUDED

ASSIGNED

ACCOSTED

DESTRUCTION

ABOUT THE AUTHOR

Katrina is a best-selling author of young adult fantasy and middle grade/tween novels. Her novels incorporate action, heart and an intriguing plot.

She resides in Queensland, Australia. Her three teenage boys and husband for over twenty-two years treat her like a princess. Unfortunately though, this princess still has to do domestic chores.

From a very young age, she has been a very creative person and has spent many years travelling the world and observing many different personalities and cultures. Her favourite personalities have been the strange ones, yet the ones under the radar also hold a place in her heart.

Katrina's online home is at www. katrinacopebooks.com
　　You can connect with Katrina on:
　　Facebook Group

facebook.com / Author.Katrina.Cope

twitter.com / Katrina_R_Cope

instagram.com / katrina_cope_author

pinterest.com / katrinacope56

bookbub.com / profile / katrina-cope